Jacqueline Davidson Kopito

TWINTASTIC
in Miami

For my Sweetie, my beautiful boys, Jared and
Jason, and my entire wonderful family
—with all my love.

PROLOGUE
Jordyn

After school, Alix and I put on some old sneakers and head upstairs to clean the attic. It's our punishment for texting in class and getting Mom and Dad called to the principal's office. I flip on the single light bulb hanging from the ceiling and look around. We've never been allowed up here before, and now I can see why. Our house is super old—it's been in Mom's family for over a hundred years—and the attic is a hot, dusty, creepy mess.

There's junk everywhere—old books, photo albums, newspapers, and trunks scattered all over the floor. The big window in the corner is covered by these torn, faded purple velvet curtains. A small, cracked table sits near the window, and the floor creaks under my feet as I tiptoe around.

On the table, there's this old diary and a big gold jewelry box that looks really fancy. The box squeaks when I slowly open it, and suddenly, this weird glowing light fills the room. Alix comes over, and we both peek inside. It's full of these colorful crystals. We each pick one up and rub them—they're super smooth.

BOOM! Out of nowhere, lightning flashes right outside, and then a loud thunderclap.

What the heck?! The sun was literally shining like two seconds ago, and now everything's gone totally bananas! The light bulb starts flickering and then the window cracks! Glass shatters everywhere, and the curtains are whipping around like crazy.

And then, get this—the diary literally floats off the table and just hangs in the air, right in front of us!

I totally freak out and grab onto Alix, clutching the green crystal like my life depends on it. Then, all the dust in the attic—on the books, newspapers, everything—just swirls up and flies out the window. The jewelry box slams shut, and the light disappears. Now there's purple smoke everywhere.

I feel this weird tingly feeling, like, all the way down to my bones.

The diary drops back to the table with a loud thud, and we stare at each other, frozen. Then, everything goes still. The wind stops, the thunder and lightning are gone, and the sun comes back through the broken window. And the purple fog disappears.

"What just happened?" I whisper-shout.

"I don't know Jordyn, but did you feel some weird energy in your body?" Alix whispers back, looking freaked out too.

"Yeah." I'm still shaking, but at least she felt it, too.

"Can science even explain this?" I ask as the light finally stops flickering.

Alix shakes her head and hands me her ruby crystal. "Maybe it's these."

I clutch it tighter. "I'm scared."

"Girls! Time for dinner!" Grandma calls from downstairs.

"Coming!" I yell, shoving the crystals in my pocket.

"On our way!" Alix shouts.

"Grab the diary—whatever you can!"

"Got it!" Alix says, arms stuffed with newspapers.

"Hurry!" I race down the stairs, and Alix is right behind me.

A few weeks later...

So, it turns out, Alix and I have magical powers! All the

identical twins in our family have had them for generations. Rubbing those crystals in the attic woke up our powers. Now we're learning to use them to help good people and stop bad people. Whenever we use our powers, tiny gold stars that look like glitter confetti float around us. It's so awesome, and only we can see them.

But here's the thing—having powers is a huge secret. Nobody knows except for Grandma. Somehow, she just knew that after we went up to the attic, we'd come down with the powers. Alix and I haven't told Mom and Dad because when we figured it out, they were super stressed with the family restaurant. We didn't want to make things worse. Even though things are better now, we're still keeping it a secret. Grandma thinks it's best for now.

Alix and I are trying to be responsible with our powers, but sometimes… things don't always go as planned.

VACATION
DAY ONE
Jordyn

"**A**lllix! Over here!" I yell, waving my arms like crazy. She walks over in her navy swimsuit, spreading her towel on the chair next to mine and dropping her dark green knapsack on the ground. "Jordyn, do you have to shout like that?"

"I wanted to make sure you saw me."

She sits down and checks her phone. "We got a group text from Dylan, Grace, and Nikki. They miss us."

"Already!"

Alix and I are in Miami for the holiday break because Dad's an incredible chef, and the D Hotel begged him to come cook and help run Kehler's, their fancy three-star restaurant. The best part? Alix and I get to stay in this super cool, super fancy suite! Meanwhile, Mom and Grandma are back home running Ace, our family restaurant.

I grab my phone and quickly text back our besties, telling them we miss them too, even though we just left. Then I practically drown myself in sunblock—better safe than sorry!

Suddenly, this tall, skinny guy with black curls walks up to us. He's holding a tray with drinks and French fries, and he's staring at us like he's trying to figure something out.

"Twins!" he says, like it's the most amazing thing ever.

"Yep," I reply, and Alix just nods like, really?

"You must be Chef Phillip's daughters! He's been bragging

about you two nonstop," he says with a grin. "You girls really are twins—same smile and everything. I'm Billy, the head waiter. I work with your dad most evenings."

Alix and I are in 6th grade, and we have long, wavy dark hair—though mine gets super frizzy sometimes— and fair skin. People always think we look the same, but trust me, we're really different.

"Hey, I'm Jordyn and this is Alix," I say, while Alix just grins. "Nice to meet you."

"Nice to meet you too," Billy replies. "Can I get you girls anything to eat or drink?"

"Ooh, I'd love an iced tea."

"Same," Alix adds, tugging at the brim of her white baseball cap.

"Two iced teas coming right up!" Billy zooms off.

"This is the best, right?!" I say, sinking into my comfy lounge chair and gazing at the insanely awesome resort. "Chilling by the pool, cold drinks being delivered to us—total perfection."

"So good," Alix agrees just as my phone pings.

"Yeeesss! It's Jackson." I can't help grinning. This day just keeps getting better and better!

Jackson's my boyfriend back home. We've been together for a couple of months.

"I didn't ask who texted you, Jordyn," Alix says, flipping open her Kindle.

"I thought you'd care." She so doesn't get what it's like to be in a relationship. Why do I even bother?

"Not really," she mumbles, already reading.

I shrug and stand up to snap a selfie for Jackson, signing off with a pink heart. He texts me back in seconds.

JACKSON

He's the cutest! I took some more pics and posted the best one on Insta. I mean, why not? I look awesome in my pink bikini. I type in the caption: Fantastic day! #Miami #Funtimes #Bikiniday, making sure to use some cool hashtags so everyone can see.

Just then, two girls in oversized sunglasses stop in front of us.

"Hey, have you seen our orange raft?" asks one girl, who's wearing a bunch of bracelets and holding a big red case.

"Nope, sorry." I shake my head as I sit back down, and Alix does the same.

"I'm Blair Takahashi and this is my little sister, Joy. She's in fifth grade—just one year younger than me, but everyone says I look a lot older. You can decide for yourself."

Joy smiles shyly. She's got these cute fuchsia slides with embroidered tropical birds on them.

"Hi, I'm Alix. And that's Jordyn," Alix says, pointing to me as I give a small wave.

I check them out. Blair definitely looks older than Joy. They're both about the same height with super shiny, straight black hair, but Blair has this grown-up vibe, while Joy's got these adorable dimples.

"Where are you from?" Joy asks all politely. "We've never seen you here before."

"It's our first time," I say, putting down my phone.

Alix chimes in. "We're from Connecticut."

"Our family comes here every year for Christmas. We love it," Blair says, adjusting her sparkly white beach cover up. "We're from the city."

"What city?" I ask, tilting my head.

"New York City," Blair says with a smirk. "Ever hear of it?"

"Uh, yeah," I say, putting on some Chapstick. Is she trying to make me feel dumb? Who does she think she is?

"I'd love to visit the Big Apple again." Alix closes her Kindle.

"Not only is it our first time here, but it's also actually our first time on a plane."

"For real?" Blair giggles. "Joy and I fly all over the world with our parents."

"Paris, Japan, Texas, California—" Joy starts listing.

Blair cuts her off. "You name it, we've been there, and we always stay at the nicest hotels, like this one."

"That's cool," Alix says, smiling.

"Are you twins?" Blair asks, looking between Alix and me.

"Yup," I answer.

"That's what I thought," Blair says. "I can see the differences."

"What's in the case?" I ask, curiously.

"My artwork." Blair opens it right away and shows us her art pad. She's got these amazing paintings of jewelry, colorful sneakers, and perfume bottles. As she's showing us, a bright yellow piece of paper falls out.

"You're really talented," Alix says, picking up the paper. I lean in to see it too.

"I like to paint landscapes," I say.

"I've been taking art classes since elementary school," Blair replies. "You can keep the flyer—I've got extras."

"Oh, cool!" I say, my eyes scanning the paper. "Whoa, an art contest for tweens?!"

"Yeah! It's on Lincoln Road, and Kennedy's Art Gallery is hosting it," Blair says, sounding all excited. "Kennedy is, like, an art god!"

"When's the contest?" I ask.

"New Year's Eve Day, at noon. It says it at the bottom." Blair points it out. "You can paint anything about nature or the holiday spirit. The winner gets five hundred dollars and a free online art class from Kennedy himself."

"I totally want to enter!" I grab the flyer from Alix. I have no idea who this Kennedy guy is, but he sounds important.

"I won last year," Blair says proudly as she zips her case.

My eyebrows shoot up as Joy's phone beeps.

"We gotta go. Mom and Dad are waiting for us to have lunch," Joy says.

"See ya around," Blair says, flipping her black hair off her shoulders as they walk away.

"Bye. I'll be on the lookout for the raft," Alix calls after them.

"They seem really cool," Alix says.

"I guess." I shove the flyer in my metallic knapsack. "But Blair seems kind of—snobby. Don't you think so?"

"Not really," Alix says, shaking her head.

"Okay, maybe snobby isn't the word—"

"Relax, Jordyn!" Alix interrupts, rolling her eyes.

"I have to enter the art contest. I need to win!" I burst out.

"Did you bring your paint stuff?"

"Of course. I might be low on a few colors, but first I have to figure out what to paint." I wonder if I should use my powers...

"You'll figure it out," Alix says.

"Mm-hmm."

Just then, Billy shows up with our iced teas, and we thank him.

Alix takes a sip and gives me a look. "Jordyn. Don't even think about it."

I blink. "What?"

"You know what. Using our powers for the contest."

Day One
Evening
Jordyn

As soon as I get back to the room, I grab my phone and Google Kennedy's Art Gallery while Alix heads to the bathroom to wash up. Tons of pictures pop up—him standing next to his paintings, holding awards, and smiling at fancy events. Whoa! Kennedy's like an art rock star. His stuff is insane— animals, people, cities—every single piece is next-level. Winning his contest would be huge. I have to win.

I change out of my bikini into a yellow tank top and jean shorts, then flop onto the bed and check Insta.

"Oh. My. God!" I shout, reading the comments out loud. "Snow White! Get a Tan! Pasty Legs!" My heart drops. I set my phone down on the bed and look away, blinking fast as my throat starts to tighten.

"What's wrong?" Alix asks, stepping out of the bathroom with her toothbrush still in her mouth. She's already dressed for dinner.

"I posted a selfie earlier, and now there's so much negativity!" I grab my phone again, my stomach twisting as more mean comments pop up. "Ghostly. Girl, get in the sun—"

"Just ignore it," Alix says, cutting me off. "Haters are going to hate."

"I wish I could, but it actually hurts! I care what other people think."

"It's just a bunch of opinions, Jordyn," Alix says, setting her toothbrush on the counter. "Why let it get to you?"

"But it's so mean!" I swallow the lump in my throat. A tiny part of me wonders—would it be so bad to use our powers for just a little tan?

Okay, okay so let me back up and tell you how Alix and I got our magical powers. A couple of months ago, we were cleaning the attic and found these cool shiny crystals that used to belong to our great-grandma Rose and her twin sister Molly (They were our grandma's mom and aunt, BTW). And get this— they were identical twins, just like us. And they totally had magical powers too. I guess it's like, a thing in our family for twins.

Anyway, when we rubbed the crystals, BAM! The powers were passed down to us. We learned all about it from this super old diary of Rose's, a bunch of random newspaper articles, and this weird book called, *Magical Powers for Twins* we found up there. I mean, who knew attics could be so cool.

So basically, Alix and I can hear each other's thoughts in our heads and move stuff with our minds. If we concentrate hard enough, we can make our thoughts come true. Rose's diary says we must work together, or else things get messy.

Right before we left for Miami, Alix and I found Molly's diary in the attic too. I haven't read it yet—and I left it at home. How could I forget?

"Jordyn let's go eat," Alix says, pulling me out of my thoughts.

"I'm not hungry."

"C'mon, we'll see Dad." Alix opens the door. "Get up!"

I drag myself out of bed and follow Alix to Kehler's. The place is really fancy—white walls like our suite, dark wood floors, and big windows. Tiny blue candles flicker on the tables, and fresh flowers are everywhere. Chill music plays in the background. I totally get why this place is so popular.

We don't have a reservation, but Alix tells the maître d´ who our dad is, and just like that, we get the VIP treatment—seated right away.

We start looking at the menus, and my eyes go wide. Everything is so expensive!

"Hey, girls! Tonight, your dad's special is the lobster salad with a skirt steak," Billy says. "And Dad told you it's all on the house, right? You should get the chocolate souffle, too."

"Sure," Alix says, as I nod. "We'll take the special and the souffle."

"Excellent choice. I'll let Dad know you're here." Billy takes the menus and heads to the kitchen.

Someone else comes by and pours ice water into our glasses. I check my phone and see that I've got more views on Insta, which makes me feel a bit better until I see more awful comments—thumbs down and a face vomiting. Ugh! I slowly sink into my chair. "Everyone is so cruel."

"Give it a rest, Jordyn."

"How can you say that? Don't you see how upset I am?" I frown.

"If you put yourself out there, you have to expect some people to say mean things," Alix says, shrugging.

"Yeah, well, that's an understatement!" I grumble, taking a sip of the cold water. "Can we please use our powers so I can get a tan. Please! Pleaseplease! Pul-leeeeez!"

"Forget it!" Alix says, firmly.

"But it's really important to me!"

Alix shakes her head. "Stop talking, Dad's coming."

Dad walks over, wearing his usual chef outfit—white jacket, black pants, and that tall white hat.

"How're my girls?" Dad asks. "I heard you met Billy. Good guy. I'm helping him train to be a line cook."

"Yeah, he's cool," I say, forcing a smile.

Alix jumps in, "Everything's great!"

"I'm glad to hear. I've got to get back to the kitchen—it's a busy night. Don't stay up too late," Dad says before rushing off.

As soon as he's gone, I turn to Alix. "C'mon, pleeeease help me! I need a tan, and our powers work way better when we use them together."

"Jordyn. NO! We don't use our powers for dumb stuff. Did you already forget your whole hair disaster?"

I roll my eyes. A few months ago, I tried to use the powers by myself to make my hair straight and silky because I was so done with the frizz. But I totally screwed it up, and my hair exploded into this giant, curly mess. Biggest fail ever!

"That was different, Alix. And I'm over my hair." I take another sip of the water. "But this is serious—I'm getting roasted!"

Alix pulls out a small, old looking book from her knapsack.

"You brought Molly's diary!"

"Obviously!" Alix hands it to me. "Read this page."

January - 1926

Dear Diary,

Rose and I are very lucky to be gifted with these magical powers. We must use them wisely to help others, not for silly things like cleaning our room. Though I must confess; Rose and I did do that once. It saved us time and energy but once is enough.

Oh dear, I must go, Rose is calling me for dinner.

Molly

"See? Use wisely and for helping people." Alix takes the diary and shoves it back in her knapsack.

"I get it, but—"

Before I can finish, Blair and Joy come over to our table. Blair is wearing a sparkly black top with black shorts, and Joy has a cute red tee shirt dress. I must admit, they look really stylish.

"Are we going to see you everywhere we go?" Blair says with a smirk.

"Hi!" Alix blurts out, totally ignoring the question and just staring at Blair. Meanwhile, I slap on the fakest smile ever.

"Nice to see you again," Joy says, all friendly.

"Yeah, really nice," Alix adds, still staring. Like, seriously?

"We'll probably be here every night since our dad is the guest chef," I say, shrugging. "And it's free."

"That's cool," Joy replies.

"Did you find the raft you were looking for?" Alix asks, sounding way too interested.

"Yeah, a lifeguard had it," Blair responds. "Thanks for asking."

"Sure," Alix mumbles, her face turning pink. Oh. My. God. What is going on with her?

Just then, Billy shows up with our food. "*Bon Appetit*, girls."

"We should be going. I don't want to keep our parents waiting. Dad has been working all the time," Blair says, looking at Alix. "See ya at the pool tomorrow."

"Definitely," Alix says, grinning as they walk away.

I glance at her and —yep, she's giggling to herself. Whatever. I've got bigger problems. Like figuring out how to get a tan without, you know, actually sunbathing. Last time I tried that, I ended up looking like a boiled lobster. Not cute. I'll figure it out. Somehow.

DAY TWO
EARLY MORNING
Alix

I look at the flyer Jordyn left on the dresser and smile. Meeting Blair and Joy yesterday was so fun. They've been to so many places around the world, which is pretty cool. And Blair is very smart, like nobody I've ever met. I can't wait to see her at the pool later.

Jordyn bursts into the room, holding two Dunkin iced teas. "Alix, I got you extra lemon."

"Thanks!" I grab my drink.

"Before we hit the pool, can we go to Lincoln Road? Grandma gave me some money. I need paint and a poster at Wendell's Art store." Jordyn slurps her drink.

Wendell's is a chain store. We have one in Connecticut down the street from our house. They have every art supply you could imagine.

"Sure. Any idea what you're going to paint?"

"Yep. But I'm still figuring out all the details," Jordyn says, taking another big slurp.

"Cool."

Jordyn's really talented. A couple of months ago, she redesigned the menus for Ace—and everyone loved them.

I grab my knapsack, and we head to the store. It's a quick walk. Jordyn goes straight to the paint aisle, and I wander around looking at the paint brushes. They have so many—flat ones, angled ones, foam ones. It's cool how many different kinds there are.

I pick one up but then notice a girl with bright red hair slipping four brushes into her brown leather bag while talking on her phone. I sneak closer and hear.

Redhead: "I just grabbed some brushes and threw them into my Gucci."

I try not to stare.

Redhead: "I mean, I could buy all of these with my trust fund, but it's fun seeing what I can get away with."

I glance around, checking to see if anyone else notices—good, it's only me.

Redhead: "I'm going to the makeup store next. Catch ya later."

I shoot a thought to Jordyn right away: *I just saw a girl steal some brushes. We have to do something.*

Jordyn sends me a thought: *Okay.*

We go back and forth with ideas, then come up with a plan. I remind her not to rush.

She finds me in the brush aisle and sends me another thought: *Let's do this!*

Tiny gold stars pop up all around the store—sparkling everywhere. But only we can see them.

The redhead trips and lands right on her butt. Thud! Everything flies out of her bag—lip gloss, phone, wallet, and the stolen brushes.

A saleslady hurries over. "Are you okay?"

"Yeah," the redhead mumbles. She grabs her stuff while the saleslady picks up the brushes.

"I'll ring these up for you," the saleslady offers.

The redhead backs away. "Don't bother." She runs out of the store.

The saleslady scratches her head and puts the brushes back.

"Perfect job," I say proudly. "Nobody steals when we're

around."

"Couldn't agree more," Jordyn adds, holding a couple of small paint cans.

We then grab a big 24 x 36 canvas poster and head to the checkout.

"I can't wait to start working on my painting." Jordyn takes the poster board while I carry the paints.

"You've got tons of time," I tell her as we walk out.

Jordyn takes a last sip of her drink. "I have to win."

We toss our empty cups in the trash. Suddenly, a guy on a bike yells, "Get a tan!"

I give him a dirty look while Jordyn stares at the ground. "These people are the worst!" she says loudly. "I'm so embarrassed. Can't we use our powers?!" Then she holds up her pale arm like it's some kind of disaster.

I shake my head. "No! Stop bugging me."

Jordyn huffs and sets down the poster. Then she clasps her hands together and goes full drama queen. "Pleeease, Alix!"

I give her a look. "We can't use our powers every time someone's mean. Forget what people think—it's their problem, not yours!"

Jordyn lets out the biggest sigh. "Oohkaay," she mumbles as the doorman opens the big glass door.

Cold air blasts as we walk inside, and Jordyn shivers.

DAY TWO
MID-MORNING
Jordyn

"**N**oooo!" I scream, louder than I ever have before.

"What's going on?" Alix comes running into the bathroom, and when she sees me, her mouth drops open like she saw a ghost.

"Don't even say it!" I grab the liquid soap, pour it all over my arms, and start scrubbing like crazy with a washcloth.

"You look like a cheese doodle!" Alix says, staring at me like I am some sort of alien.

"All those comments and emojis were so mean! I just wanted a nice bronze tan," I say, continuing to scrub even harder.

"Don't listen to the haters!"

"Easy for you to say, but it's not coming off!"

"So, this is my fault now?"

"I didn't say that," I mutter, scrubbing until my arms hurt. "Can we use our powers to fix this?"

Alix shakes her head. "I'm going to the pool."

"I can't believe you won't help! I'm your one and only twin," I shout as Alix slams the door behind her.

Suddenly, I hear my cell. It's Jackson, FaceTiming me. "Oh no!" I gasp. I quickly dry my hands, and I look in the mirror. Ugh! I think fast and turn off the light so there's just a little daylight coming through the window. Maybe I won't look as orange. I check the mirror again. Not too bad—I hoped. Then I tap on.

"Hi! What's up?" I say, fluffing up my hair.

"Did you lay out or something?" Jackson asks.

"Yeah, something like that—"

"The Miami life is really getting to you." Jackson laughs.

"I guess." If only he knew the truth, I think to myself.

"I want to come and see you for New Year's Eve. My Uncle Charlie has a place near your hotel. I'll check if I can stay with him. Is that cool?"

"That would be awesome!" My orangish skin better be gone by then.

Jackson smiles as I hear his mom in the background. "Hold on a sec."

While I wait, I glance down at my orange legs. I feel horrible. No—worse than horrible. Using these powers really backfired.

"I gotta go—Mom's taking me to soccer," Jackson says. "Miss you, girlfriend."

"Miss you too!" I say and click off. Just then, I get a text from Alix.

Why am I being so nice to Alix anyway. If she just agreed to use the powers in the first place, I wouldn't be in this mess. But—okay, fine. It's kind of my fault. Actually, it's *totally* my fault. I was being selfish. And now I look like a giant cheese puff!

DAY TWO
AFTERNOON
Alix

I'm sitting by the pool alone since Jordyn couldn't come. I'm trying to read on my Kindle, but it's hard for me to focus. I keep thinking about Blair. I look around, but she's not here. Maybe she changed her mind. I need to stop overthinking. Right when I get back to reading, Blair taps my foot, surprising me.

"Hi!" she says, slipping off her flip-flops and dropping her beach bag right next to my lounge chair.

"Finally, you're here!" I blurt out—and then immediately wish I could take it back.

"I was coding all morning," she says, pushing her sunglasses up.

"What are you working on?" I ask, closing my Kindle.

"I'm building an app—it's called Ask Blair. People can ask me anything about painting, and I give tips and stuff. I'm also finding cool young artists to feature." Blair leans back in her chair.

"Impressive," I say, leaning back too. Now we're facing each other as she keeps talking about her app. She's got such a nice smile.

"Thanks, but it's no big deal. Everyone at my school is working on something cool," she says like it's completely normal.

My eyes widen. I took a beginner coding class once, but I'm nowhere near her level. "What school do you go to?" I ask.

"Pence. It's an all-girls private school. You've heard of it, right?"

I shake my head slowly, feeling out of my league.

"Seriously? It's one of the top schools in the whole country." Blair giggles. "That's actually kind of cute you haven't heard of it."

I giggle too, and pretty soon we're both laughing—even though I'm not sure why. Then Billy walks over.

"Hello, young ladies. No sisters today," he asks with a smile. "What can I get you?"

"Joy's out shopping with Mom, and Dad's working," Blair says. "I'll have a Cobb salad and a bottled water."

"Good choice. And for you?" Billy asks, waiting patiently.

I'm thrown off that Blair ordered a salad. I never ordered one before, and neither have any of my friends back home. It's so grown-up. I was going to get grilled cheese and fries, but I quickly change my mind.

"I'll have the same," I say politely.

Billy nods. "I'll be back soon."

"He's so nice," I say, watching him take another order nearby.

"I don't really know him. He's new here, but he seems helpful," Blair says, glancing at my Kindle. "What are you reading?"

"Astronomy. I love learning all about the sun, moon, planets, and stars."

"Me too!"

Finally! Something we have in common. "Cool."

From then on, we talk non-stop about space, hobbies, school, and museums. Even when Billy brings our food, we keep talking.

"My parents got me a telescope a few weeks ago," Blair says. "Every night, I go on my balcony and look at the stars."

"Amazing!" I say. "Do you live in a tall apartment building?"

"Yeah."

"Ever use it to stargaze or spy on people?" I ask, giggling.

Blair laughs. "One time I accidentally saw some guy tossing a pie at someone during an argument. It was a whole mess."

"Yikes! I would stick to the stars from now on."

"Exactly!" Blair grins.

After a while, Blair gets a text. "Mom's upset," she says, texting back quickly.

"Everything okay?"

"Should be." Blair finishes texting. "I can't believe it's almost dinner."

"I know. This was so much fun!"

Blair grabs her bag and puts on her flip-flops. "We have to do this again."

"Tomorrow?" I ask—maybe a little too excited.

She smiles. "Sure thing." Then she takes off her sunglasses and looks right at me. "*Ciao.*"

I wave goodbye, feeling my cheeks turning pink.

As Blair walks away, I can't stop smiling. I know we just met, but it feels like we've been friends forever. She really gets me.

DAY THREE
MORNING
Jordyn

When I wake up, Alix is reading in bed. I rush to the bathroom to check myself out.

"It's fading! Don't you think I look better? I'm not so orange. Riiight?" I yell as I run back into the bedroom.

"Can't we talk about this later?" Alix's eyes are glued to Molly's diary.

I flip on the lights. "Didn't it get better?"

Alix barely moves her head. "Yeah."

"You're not even looking."

"Okay." Alix sits up and stares at me. "There's a bit of improvement."

"Exactly," I say as Grandma FaceTimes us. I grab my phone, plop down on Alix's bed, and answer it.

"What happened to your skin?" Grandma asks, wearing her favorite lavender cardigan.

Grandma's lived with us since we were little. She's always there making sure we eat enough, finish our homework, and just… taking care of us. Especially when Mom and Dad are working, which feels like all the time.

"Good morning," I say in a sing-songy voice.

"I don't see Alix," Grandma says.

"Here I am," Alix says, moving closer to me.

"Now I can see both my twinnies. Jordyn, are you going to tell me what happened?"

"I tried to use my powers to get a tan, but it didn't go well."

"Consequences, Jordyn. Consequences," Grandma says in her serious tone.

"Uh-huh," I say, sinking into the pillows.

Grandma knows all about these powers since her mom was Rose.

"Are you meeting any new friends?" Grandma asks.

"Yep," Alix answers, smiling.

"We're having a blast," I say. Well, I was—until I turned orange.

"I'm glad you're having fun and meeting nice people," Grandma says, sipping her tea. "I have to help Mom at the restaurant. It's been busy. I just wanted to check in. Love you both."

"Bye, Grandma. Talk soon!" I say.

Alix adds, "Love you."

Grandma blows kisses and taps off.

"How was hanging with Blair yesterday? I forgot to ask," I say.

"Great."

"You don't think she's a bit of a know-it-all?"

"No way. I'm expanding myself by spending time with her," Alix says. "She's working on this cool app."

"Expaaaanding yourself?" I say, rolling my eyes. I don't even ask about the app. This conversation is making my stomach churn.

"Yeah, that's right," Alix says firmly.

What's with her? Alix never talks like this. She's being super annoying.

Ping! My phone goes off. Then Alix's. Nikki's text pops up, and we dive right in.

Nikki

> *Mom made her famous Gulab Jamuns when Dylan and Grace came over last night. I know how much u love it.* 😃

Jordyn

> *Yummyeeee!* 😋

Gulab Jamuns are this amazing Indian dessert—fried milk balls soaked in sweet syrup. Nikki's mom, Mrs. Oberio, is from India, and she makes the best food.

Alix

> *Wish I could have some now! Miss You.* 🖤

We all text goodbye, and I put my phone away.

"Busy morning," I say, stretching. "I can't go to the pool today. I have to work on my painting."

"Did you sign up and print the form?" Alix asks, peeking outside.

"Don't look! I need to finish it." I quickly close the drapes. "I still have to register."

"There's a computer in the lobby that guests can use," Alix says. "Then we can visit Dad and get some breakfast."

"Sounds like a plan." I throw on sweats even though it's super hot—gotta hide my orange skin. Then I pat some powder on my face to tone it down. Not too bad.

"Ready," I say. As Alix and I grab our knapsacks and leave our suite, we hear someone scream. We rush down the hall and find a guest with her door wide open, freaking out.

"My baby finch! I let her out of her cage, and she flew away," the guest says, almost crying.

Alix runs to the lobby and yells, "She's close to the ceiling!"

I catch up and look up at the bird. Alix's thoughts come to me: *We need to use our powers. It's the only way to rescue her.*

I send my thought back: *Agreed!*

Alix's thoughts continue: *Remember to concentrate, visualize, and don't rush. Pause. That's what the Magical Powers Book says.*

We focus together: *We must save the cute little birdie.*

Magical gold stars float around in the lobby. Suddenly, I'm holding the finch in my hands and Alix starts petting her.

The guest runs over, "My baby. Thank you!" She takes the bird from me. "You're both angels!"

"You're welcome," we say, smiling.

She hugs us and goes back happily to her room.

"Great-aunt Molly would be proud," I say, standing in front of the computer.

"Yep, and so would great-grandma Rose," Alix says, pulling out the diary from her knapsack. She hands me a newspaper article.

"Remember how we found those newspaper clippings in the attic? Molly's diary has some that we never read," Alix explains. "Look at this one."

Gazette News

February – 1926

Local twins and junior high school students Rose and Molly Davis ended up in the right place at the right time. On Thursday afternoon, they happened upon their former gym teacher, Mr. Darpino, standing with a neighbor just outside Franklin Elementary School. Seems the local neighbor's kitten wouldn't come down from the athletic shed's roof outside the school.

As Mr. Darpino and the neighbor ran to get a ladder, the twins stayed behind to keep watch over the frightened kitty. By the time they returned, the twins were holding the fluffy little kitten in their arms.

Thanks Rose and Molly!

"We're just like them, helping anyone we can."

"Well, most of the time, Jordyn," Alix says, staring at my orangish hands.

I give her a half smile and hand back the article. I type on the computer, Kennedyartcontest.com, fill out the form, press print and tell myself I'm going to win!

The clerk hands me the printed paper, and I put it in my knapsack. Alix and I head into Kehler's, but it's empty. I don't see the maître d' or anyone. "Let's find Dad. He's probably in the kitchen."

"I hope we don't get into trouble," Alix says softly.

"It'll be fine," I say, even though I'm not sure. The place feels eerie. Where is everyone? Then I spot Billy. Wait—what?

"Billy's stealing!" I whisper-shout, my eyes wide.

He's in the far corner of the kitchen, pulling money out of the safe and stuffing it in an envelope. I look at Alix, and she silently mouths, "Let's get out of here!"

We sneak out fast and bump right into Dad in the dining area. Good thing the lights are dim—otherwise he'd totally notice my orange glow.

"Girls! What's going on?" Dad laughs, carrying grocery bags. "We don't open until 10:00 AM. Didn't you see the sign?"

"Um, I guess not," I say, a bit nervous. "You're not gonna believe this!"

"It's okay. The door was opened when I came in. Maybe someone forgot to lock up last night. Or maybe one of the staff members is in the back," Dad says. "I can whip you up some eggs if you want."

"No, thanks. We're just happy to see you," Alix says calmly. "By the time you get back to the suite, we're usually asleep, and you're gone before sunrise."

"It's been busy here. I appreciate you looking out for one another. Are you sure you don't want any breakfast? It's no trouble," Dad says, shifting the bags around.

"We're not really hungry," I say as Alix and I exchange looks.

"Okay, let me get this food in the fridge. I have to prep some new dishes. Billy is assisting me," Dad says. "Did you know he's the hotel manager's nephew?"

"Nope," I say, shaking my head. Alix does the same.

"The manager is a tough guy, and he treats Billy like his own kid," Dad explains. "I wouldn't want to cross Billy or his uncle if I want to be asked back next year."

"Yeah," I say as Alix and I exchange more looks.

"This job is really important for me." Dad checks his watch. "I need to get going soon. Jordyn, was there something you wanted to tell me."

"Umm…nah, it's nothing."

"Okay, then. See you later, my beautiful, brilliant daughters."

We both laugh.

The second we step out of the restaurant; Alix and I sprint back to our room.

"I wanted to tell Dad," I say, catching my breath.

Alix groans, rubbing her forehead. "I wanted to tell Dad too, but now that we know Billy is the manager's nephew, it's not a good idea."

"What do we do now?" I ask, looking at her.

Alix sighs. "I think we need proof before we tell Dad."

"Yeah," I reply. "We can't put Dad in a tough spot."

After thinking for a bit, Alix says, "I have an idea. I was reading Molly's diary, and there's a new power we could use."

"What is it?"

Alix pulls out the diary, turns to the middle, and shows me the page.

February - 1926

Dear Diary,

     Today, Rose and I learned we had a new magical power when we were ice skating on the pond. Rose was way ahead of me, so I yelled, "Freeze." Rose stopped, but the funniest thing happened. All the kids around us froze-in -time. Rose and I couldn't believe our eyes and we were laughing. Then, Rose yelled, "Un-freeze." Everyone started skating again. We did this a bunch of times and figured out we can freeze people in time for up to one minute. I think this power will be very useful.

I'm going to have some hot chocolate with some sugar cookies that Rose made.

Bye for now.

Molly

"Woo-hoo! This power is so cool!" I yell, practically jumping up and down. "But how's this gonna help us catch Billy stealing?"

"Next time we see him in action, we'll use it," Alix says. "And—"

I cut her off. "Wait—what do you mean exactly?"

"Let me explain," Alix says, leaning in. "When we catch him stealing, we freeze him, snap a pic, and boom—we have proof. It'll be quick. Then, before we leave, we'll un-freeze him like nothing happened. After that, we show the pic to Dad, and he can tell the hotel security or call the cops."

I blink. "That's actually genius. But how do we know when he's gonna steal again?"

"We just have to be on the lookout," Alix says.

"So basically, we need to check on him whenever the kitchen's closed—or maybe even when it's open."

"We'll be like Young Sherlock Holmes!" Alix giggles.

I crack up. "Okay, that was a good one."

Once we stop laughing, I grin. "Now, let's raid the mini fridge and find some snacks!"

DAY THREE
AFTERNOON
Jordyn

lix goes to the pool while I'm basically melting in my sweats. I give up and change into my shorts and my splash shirt—my favorite oversized tee with paint splatters all over it. I wear it every time I paint.

It's so hot, and since no one's around, I don't mind showing my legs today. I head out to the patio under the blue awning, where my painting stuff is set up. My landscape is coming along, but I still have a ton to do before the contest.

Then I hear kids splashing at the pool. I look over—Blair's hugging Alix like they're besties. Of course, she is. She bugs me so much. I can't wait to beat her in the contest.

After painting for a while, I hear my phone. It's Jackson on FaceTime. Oh no! I don't want him seeing me like this in broad daylight with my weird orange skin. I sprint inside, grab my sunglasses, and start searching for my blue bucket hat with pink flowers. The room is a total mess, but I finally find it under the chair. I shove it on my head, run back outside, and answer.

"Hey Jackson," I say, twirling a piece of my hair.

"Cute hat, Curly!" He grins.

"Thanks," I say, feeling so clever for hiding my face under it.

"It's snowing here. Soccer got cancelled." He sighs.

"That stinks."

He nods and takes a big sip from his Hydro Flask. "I still haven't heard back from Uncle Charlie."

"I really hope you can come for New Year's!"

"Me too."

He takes another sip. "Why aren't you at the pool?"

"I'm working on a painting."

We talk until he has to go shovel snow.

"Later, Curly!"

I laugh to myself. Jackson still calls me Curly after my whole hair disaster, which is so cute. I hope he visits, and I really hope my orange skin is gone by then!

I glance around—there's Billy by the pool, all Mr. Nice Guy. Alix and I know better. He's a crook. Don't let the smile fool you; he can't be trusted!

Then I see Blair splashing in the pool with a girl who I think is Joy. But wait—it's Alix! What? She hates pools. I'm so confused.

I head back inside, turn on the TV, and start cleaning up. A commercial pops up with models who have fair skin—like me (well, like I was before I turned into a cheese puff). I remind myself of Alix's advice—don't let haters get to you. I've got to let go and just accept myself.

After a while, Alix comes in and chucks her bag onto the floor with a loud thud. She heads straight for the bathroom and yells, "How's the painting?"

I put down the diary. "I'm totally gonna win the contest!"

"Can we have dinner with Blair and Joy tonight?" Alix asks, popping her head out of the bathroom like she didn't even hear me.

I hesitate. "Um—"

"It'll be fun!" she says, cutting me off before disappearing back inside. A second later, I hear the shower turn on.

Great. Now I have to eat with Blair. Just great.

Alix

Before Jordyn and I enter Kehler's, we see Billy in the lobby laughing with a big man dressed in a fancy suit with slicked back gray hair.

"Hey, Alix and Jordyn!" Billy calls out. "These girls are Chef Phillip's twins," he tells the man.

"Hi," we both say politely.

"This is my Uncle Axel," Billy says, grinning.

"Love this kid like he's my own," Uncle Axel says in a deep voice, giving Billy a playful slap on the back. "How's it going?"

"Good," I say, while Jordyn just stands there, kind of quiet.

"Your Pop is a terrific chef!" Uncle Axel adds. "Glad he came on board."

"Thanks," I reply as Jordyn nods.

"Enjoy your meal," Billy says.

On our way to the dining area, Jordyn leans over and whispers, "I don't know why, but that uncle is kind of scary, right?"

"Yeah," I whisper back. "We really have to catch Billy. Our plan's going to work perfectly."

"Totally," Jordyn says.

"There they are!" I smile when I spot Blair and Joy already at a table.

Blair greets me with a hug. "I'm so happy you're here."

"Me too." I sit next to her.

"I ordered a pepperoni pizza, garlic bread, and a family-sized Caesar salad for us," Blair says.

"It's good," Joy says. "I had it the other night."

"Jordyn, did you get a spray tan?" Blair asks.

"Um—" Jordyn tries to answer, but Blair cuts her off. "I don't think they did a good job."

Jordyn and I exchange a glance while she squirms in her seat. "It'll fade," I say quickly.

"I wouldn't trust any place but where I go," Blair says. "It's literally the best salon in the city on Third Avenue on the Upper East Side—right by our apartment."

"What's the Upper East Side?" I ask. Feeling clueless again. Blair laughs like it's obvious.

"The Upper East Side is the best place to live in the city—shops, restaurants, everything!" she says.

"Sounds cool," I say.

"You'll have to visit me," Blair says. "You'll love it."

"Maybe we can see a Broadway show," Joy adds. "I love musicals."

"Definitely!" I reply.

"We saw *Wicked* on a field trip in fourth grade," Jordyn mentions.

"Saw it. Great show," Blair agrees. "How's your painting? I just started mine."

"Almost done," Jordyn says proudly.

"She's really creative, just like you," I say to Blair, smiling.

Blair smirks. "I guess we'll see." Jordyn narrows her eyes and mutters, "Good luck."

The waiter with a peace tattoo on his arm drops off our food. "This looks great," I say, gulping.

"Dig in," Blair says, grabbing a slice of pizza. "My app is almost done. I can't wait till it goes live."

"That's great!" I help myself to some salad.

"I found a few more artists to feature," Blair adds, slicing up her pizza.

"What's your app about?" Jordyn asks.

"Alix didn't tell you?" Blair looks at me. "It's for painting tips —and I showcase cool kid artists."

"Interesting," Jordyn says, taking a piece of garlic bread. I glance at her, feeling bad Blair's being a bit harsh.

Blair nudges me. "Aren't you going to try the pizza?"

"Yeah, I didn't get to it yet," I say. Dinner stays awkward, and we head back to our rooms.

Jordyn and I change into our pajamas.

"Why'd you go in the pool today?" Jordyn asks. "You usually hate pools."

I shrug. "It doesn't bug me as much anymore."

Jordyn squints at me. "For real?"

I sigh. "Okay, fine. I went in because I wanted to be with Blair. I really like her."

"Like her, like her?" Jordyn asks, raising an eyebrow.

"Yeah!"

"Blair?!" Jordyn cries.

"Why are you freaking out? Is it because she's a girl?"

"NO! I don't care if you like boys or girls. I kind of already guessed you weren't into boys," Jordyn says.

"Then what's the problem?"

"She's not that nice." Jordyn gets into bed.

"Blair was kind of rude at dinner. I don't know why," I say, grabbing an extra blanket.

"And she's just so full of herself."

"This is the first girl I really like. Can you please give her a chance?" I ask, getting into my bed.

"I'll try," Jordyn says, fluffing her pillows.

"Do you think everyone from home knows?"

"Know what?"

"That I like girls," I say. "I don't want people judging me."

"I don't know, but that's your thing. Don't stress about what other people think—that's their problem. Isn't that what you always tell me."

"But it's different," I argue.

"No, it's not!" Jordyn exclaims.

"Yeah, I guess maybe you're right." I nod. "Only good vibes!"

"Totally!"

"You're not as orange—it's peachier," I say.

"Peach is good!" Jordyn grins, snuggling under her blanket. "I'm gonna crush Blair and win that contest."

"Good night, Jordyn," I say, flicking off the light.

I'm so glad I finally told her about Blair. I couldn't keep it a secret anymore. I just hope Jordyn can get along with her, because she's really cool!

DAY FOUR
MORNING
Jordyn

It's very early, and Alix and I are trying to open the door to Kehler's.

"It's locked," I whisper.

"Time for our magical powers," Alix says, grinning. "We have to catch Billy."

"On it!" I reply.

We focus hard, and little yellow stars swirl around the door.

"Open sesame," Alix says.

We sneak inside. It's dark and quiet, especially in the kitchen.

"Billy's not here," Alix whispers, peeking around.

I flick on the lights. "Ugh, dang it!"

"Come on, let's get out of here before we get caught," Alix says. "And turn off the lights!"

We hurry out and lock the door again with our powers.

"Figures," I mutter.

"We'll catch him eventually." Alix adjusts her baseball cap and tucking her hair behind her ear as we stand in the lobby.

Just then, the waiter with the peace tattoo walks by. "Waiting for Kehler's to open? We don't start serving for another hour."

"Oh! Uh, thanks for the heads up," I say, forcing a smile.

"No problem. I'm Doug, by the way. I remember you two from last night—you look so much alike."

"Yeah, we get that all the time," I say. "We're twins. I'm Jordyn and this is Alix."

Alix gives him a quick smile. "Hey."

"Nice meeting you both," Doug says as he unlocks the door to Kehler's. "Have a good one!"

Then I check my phone and see an email from Kennedy's Art Contest. I glance up and spot a clerk at the front desk. Yes—perfect! I hurry over and say, "Hi, I'm in the art contest," then quickly forward the email. "Can you print out my registration number, please?"

"Give me a few minutes," he says.

While we wait, a super fancy lady starts freaking out nearby. She's got on high heels, a giant beige sunhat, and a sparkly diamond ring.

"Where's my third suitcase?" she yells at the bellman.

"What does it look like?" he asks, staying calm.

"Like the rest of them," she snaps, pointing to the two red leather bags.

I look around, trying to help. No red suitcase in sight—until I glance outside and see it packed in the backseat of a convertible. The driver's just about to hop in.

I send a quick thought to Alix, who's chilling on a chair: *We must move that suitcase inside.*

Got it! Alix replies in thought.

Gold stars swirl above the car, and a moment later, the red suitcase appears in the lobby. I drag it over to the other bags.

"I couldn't help but overhear—"

The fancy lady cuts me off. "Finally, someone who's actually helpful!" She inspects it.

"Thanks," the bellman whispers to me, looking relieved.

"Can we get moving now," the fancy lady snaps again, marching toward the elevator.

The bellman loads all the luggage onto a shiny gold cart, then smiles at me. "You're very sweet," he says before wheeling it away.

"Happy to help!" I reply.

Alix steps up beside me. "Some people are so rude," she mutters. "But I'm glad our powers came in handy."

"Me too!"

"Here's your registration information," the clerk calls out, giving it to me.

"Thanks!" I say as Alix and I head back.

"I found another clipping in Molly's diary," Alix says while I rummage in the mini fridge for something to eat.

I grab a candy bar and read the news article.

Gazette News

March - 1926

Banks, stores, and restaurants were saved by local twins, Rose and Molly Davis. A troubled teenager turned on the fire hydrants all over town. Before the water could flood the streets, the resourceful twins shut them off and caught the troublemaker. The mayor commented, "Rose and Molly went beyond their civic duty to serve our community. We're all grateful.

Thank you twins!

"Feels good to help people, doesn't it?" Alix says, peeling her orange. "We're just like them."

"Definitely!" I say, just as Grandma FaceTimes us.

"Jordyn, are you eating chocolate first thing in the morning?" Grandma asks, frowning.

"Hi!" I say, quickly wiping my mouth.

"I'm having an orange," Alix says, holding it up to the screen.

"Good. At least one of you is eating healthy," Grandma replies. "What's new?"

"Alix has a girlfriend," I blurt out.

"Very nice!" Grandma grins.

"It's not official," Alix says.

Mom suddenly appears next to Grandma. "Did I hear that Alix has a girlfriend?"

"Hi Mom!" Alix and I say in unison.

"Can we please stop talking about my love life?" Alix groans.

"I'm excited for you," Mom says.

"Thanks!" Alix says. "How'd you know I like girls?"

"It's no surprise," Grandma says with a chuckle.

"I'm your mother," Mom says. "I just know. And what does it matter if you like guys or gals?"

"We just want you to be happy," Grandma adds.

Alix laughs.

"I got some news too," I say.

"Let's hear it." Mom waits patiently.

"I signed up for an art contest."

"That's wonderful!" Mom cheers.

"I'm sure you'll do great!" Grandma says, getting up. "Excuse me, I need to turn off my tea kettle."

"Thanks!" I yell, feeling proud.

"Jordyn, you've got a beautiful, healthy glow, but don't get too much sun," Mom warns.

"Yep! I'll be careful." Mom just made my day! Buh-bye looking like a cheese doodle—hello, sunshine glow!

"Grandma and I have to head to Ace. I'm glad I got to see my girls this morning," Mom says, waving goodbye.

Grandma returns. "Jordyn, please find something nutritional to eat," she says before clicking off.

I toss the rest of my chocolate bar in the trash. "Alix, can we go to Wendell's? I need more blue paint."

"Sure," Alix replies. "Let me text Blair."

I nod.

"Blair wants to come. She needs paint too," Alix says, grabbing her bag.

"Really?" I mutter. Then a scary thought hits me. "Is she gonna join us for everything now?"

Alix gives me a sharp look.

We meet in the lobby and head towards Wendell's. I wander around, checking out all the different shades of blue, when someone taps me on the shoulder.

I spin around fast. "Hi Jordyn!" Kate yells.

"Whoa! What are you doing here?!"

Back home, Kate was the mean girl at middle school—at least, that's what Alix and I thought. But once we actually got to know her, she wasn't a meanie after all. Now we're all friends. Oh, and guess what? She's been going out with Vaughn—aka Jackson's best friend.

"Mom and I came here to help Nana. She's getting better after hip surgery," Kate explains.

"I'm so happy you're here!" I say, giving her hug. "And I'm glad your Nana's doing better."

"Is Alix here too?" Kate asks, tucking her long, straight strawberry blond hair behind her ear.

"Yup," I say as Alix and Blair walk over.

"Kate! So good to see you," Alix says, giving her a big hug.

"Where are you staying?" she asks.

"We're at the D Hotel."

"No way! Nana's place is right down the street," Kate says grinning.

"Cool," Alix says.

"Let's take a pic." I grab my phone. "I'll send it to Nikki, Dylan and Grace."

"Great idea!" Kate laughs as we squish together. "Send it to me too."

The photo's perfect. I send it to everyone.

"Nobody's going to introduce me?" Blair asks, side-eyeing Kate and giving Alix a look.

"Hi!" Kate says, sounding very cheerful.

Blair crosses her arms. "So—how do you all know each other?"

"We go to school together," I explain, grabbing the perfect shade of blue paint.

Kate watches me. "Wait—why are you getting paint?"

"I signed up for the Kennedy's Art Contest," I say. "I need it for my painting."

"I'm doing it too!" Kate says, her eyes lighting up. "Nana used to manage the gallery, and she always wanted me to enter. I took art classes this summer, so I figured, why not?"

"This'll be my second time," Blair announces, way too loudly. "I won last year."

Ugh. Blair's always bragging. So annoying! How does Alix not notice?

Kate's eyebrows shoot up. "Oh wow, congrats!"

"Thanks," Blair says, all proud, then grabs Alix's hand and pulls her toward the register.

Kate leans toward me. "That's weird!"

"Not really," I say, following them.

After we pay, we walk outside, bags in hand. I turn to them. "Wanna get ice cream?"

Alix glances at Blair before answering. "Yeah—sure," she finally says.

"Nah, I gotta go," Kate says, rushing off.

"What's up with her?" Alix asks.

I shrug. "I have no clue."

A few minutes later, we're sitting outside the ice cream shop.

"The frozen yogurt is so delicious," Blair says, taking another bite.

Yogurt? Seriously? Why not just get a sundae? And now Alix wants yogurt too? She never even eats it. Since when does she do everything Blair does?

"Jordyn, our friends love the pic," Alix says.

I didn't even hear my phone. I pull it out, turn up the volume, and check my messages. Nikki, Dylan, and Grace sent the nicest replies.

Alix keeps scrolling. "Kate didn't say anything—not even an emoji. Do you think she didn't like how she looked or something?"

I text back a quick thanks to everyone. "Um—I have no idea." Then I take a huge spoonful of ice cream and let it melt in my mouth. So good.

"Can I see?" Blair asks.

Alix tilts her cell so Blair can look.

"You look pretty," Blair says.

"Thanks," Alix replies, smiling. "Do you want to go to the pool after this?"

"Only if you jump first," Blair teases.

"Deal."

I finish the last of my ice cream. "I'm heading back to finish my painting."

Blair smirks. "I'm definitely winning," she says like it's a fact.

"Ha! Not a chance," I shoot back. My painting's totally gonna crush it!

DAY FOUR
EARLY AFTERNOON
Alix

"**B**efore you meet up with Blair, I have to ask you something," Jordyn says.

"Sure, what's up?"

She gives me a look. "I know you and Blair are getting close," she says as I nod. "But just—don't ever, ever say anything about our powers."

I roll my eyes. "Jordyn. Do you think I'm dumb?" I put my hands on my hips. "I would never!"

"Okay, okay." Jordyn pulls out Molly's diary. "I want to show you this."

April - 1926

    Dear Diary,

    Rose and I are grateful for these marvelous powers. But it's very important that we do NOT tell a soul. If people found out, our friends at school might ask us to use the powers for their own reasons. Things could potentially get out of control and cause chaos.

"This isn't new to me." I close the diary. "Just because I'm hanging out with Blair doesn't mean I'm going to spill our secret!"

"Okaaay!" Jordyn says with a tiny smile. "I'm just reminding you, that's all."

I sigh. "All right. I got to go."

"Bye!" Jordyn shouts as I shut the door.

I meet up with Blair, and we sit on these cushy lounge chairs. Joy's already splashing around in the pool.

"Have you ever gone out with a girl before?" I ask.

Blair turns to me. "I hung out with this cool girl from California at sleepaway camp. She was a year older."

"What happened?"

"We kept in touch for a while, but it kind of faded," Blair says, pulling her shiny black hair into a ponytail.

I don't want things to fizzle between us, but I stay quiet. And sleepaway camp? I wonder what that's like. Me and my friends hang out at the beach in the summer.

I just nod while Blair starts chatting on her phone.

Then I notice Billy writing down orders with his backpack on.

"C'mon in the water!" Joy yells to us.

Blair shakes her head, and I say loudly, "Maybe later."

I grab my Kindle and start reading, but I keep glancing at Blair. She's still on her cell like I'm not even here.

Suddenly, I hear this familiar voice screaming. I look up—it's that fancy lady from the lobby.

"Where's my ring?!! Where is it?" She's running around, asking everyone, "Have you seen my diamond ring?"

"What happened?" I ask when she gets to me.

"I took it off to put on sunscreen," she says, adjusting her big sun hat. "When I went to put it back on, it was gone!"

"That's awful!" I say, taking off my baseball cap and shoving it in my knapsack. "I'm Alix, by the way. I'll keep an eye out."

"Thank you, honey. Your sister found my suitcase. If you could find my ring, I'd be grateful." She rushes off to ask someone else.

I look around but don't see any shiny ring anywhere. Blair's still glued to her phone. I'm just about to get up when she finally says something.

"Sorry about that," she says, putting it down.

"You didn't have to come if you were going to be on the phone the whole time," I say with a sigh.

"Alix, I'm really sorry." Blair squeezes my hand. "I was just talking to my mom—she's been really stressed lately. I got all worked up. It happens."

"Yeah, I get it, I guess." I look down and notice all her pretty bracelets.

"Here, I want you to have this," she says, taking off a beaded one and handing it to me.

"I accept your apology, you don't have to give me anything," I say, trying to give it back. I'm not even that into jewelry, but it's really nice of her.

"No, for real, I want you to have it," Blair insists.

"Okay, thanks," I say, sliding it onto my wrist. "I'll take good care of it."

"It's our friendship bracelet now," she says.

We both smile as Joy starts singing in the pool.

"Nothing ever stops her," Blair mutters, rolling her eyes.

Joy belts out, "It's swim time! Splishy splashy swimming! Ohhh yeah! Swimming tiiime—"

Blair groans. "See what I mean?" Then she turns to me. "Wanna go in?"

I grin. "Only if you go in first!"

We both crack up, laughing.

DAY FOUR
LATE AFTERNOON
Jordyn

"**D**one!" I say out loud, even though no one is around. I stare at my painting. It's a beach scene with a morning sky and white clouds. The ocean is calm, and you can see the sun's reflection in the water. On the sand, there's a small Christmas tree with little yellow and orange lights, a tall Hannukah menorah, and a Kwanzaa kinara. It's simple but festive.

The contest's in three days. No powers needed—I'm gonna crush it!

I head to the bathroom to wash all the brushes when Jackson pops up on FaceTime.

"Hey!"

"Bad news. Uncle Charlie's not coming back to Miami until the end of January."

"Ugh, I'll be home by then." I toss my brushes in the sink.

"Yeah, bummer."

"Anyone else you could crash with?" I ask.

He laughs. "Not really—unless I've got some secret cousin in Florida. Guess we'll just celebrate when you're back."

"Okay, sounds good." I try not to sound disappointed.

Jackson checks his watch. "Gotta run—soccer practice."

"How's it going?" I ask.

"It's intense. Tons of kids are trying out for the spring team."

"You'll make it!"

"Thanks, Curly. Later!"

I click off and let out a big sigh. I miss Jackson like crazy. Having to wait until I'm back home to see him in person? Such a letdown. Still—not his fault.

After I finish scrubbing the brushes, reading a little more of Molly's diary, and hopping in the shower, I get dressed for dinner. I pull on a pink tee and shorts, then stop and stare. I'm back to my normal color. Why did I waste my powers for a dumb tan? I mean, my legs look pretty good. This is me—and if someone doesn't like it, that's their problem.

I'm just lacing up my sneakers when Alix bursts in, totally freaking out.

"I don't know if I'm good at this whole relationship thing!"

"What do you mean?"

Alix sighs, dropping her knapsack on the floor. "Blair was on her phone the whole time at the pool. I felt ignored, so I told her."

"I get that," I say. "But she's allowed to talk to other people."

"Yeah." Alix sighs again. "I think I'm just being needy. Am I pathetic or what?"

"NO! Not at all." I shake my head. "Honestly, I think it's cool you told her how you felt."

I flop onto my bed. "One time, Jackson told me he had a soccer game, but then I saw a post of him at a pizza place. I totally freaked out and thought he lied just to hang out with his friends."

"Oh yeah, I remember you being upset," Alix says.

"Yeah, but when I asked him, he said the game got canceled and he did text me—I just never saw it."

"You're right," Alix says. "Talking stuff out is really important."

"Totally! And don't ever feel weird saying how you feel." I glance at her wrist. "Wait—where'd you get that?"

"Blair gave it to me," Alix says, holding up her arm. "It's our friendship bracelet."

"Ooooh nice!" I grin.

"Yeah…" Alix mumbles, still staring at it. "I've just never really done this kind of thing before."

"It can be kind of confusing."

Alix nods.

"Blair might not be my favorite person," I say, making a goofy face. "But I want you to be happy. I've got your back. Always."

"Same here." Alix grins, grabs the diary and flips it open. "Wait— this reminds me of something Molly wrote." She hands it to me.

April - 1926

Dear Diary,

A girl in class has been very cruel to me. I talked to Rose about it for hours. I'm so grateful to have her as my twin so I wrote a poem for our birthday.

A twin sister helps you through difficult times,

Her comforting words are much more than dimes.

A sister fills your life with laughs and smiles,

These memories will last forever and ever.

I hope she likes it. I will write more tomorrow.

Bye for now.

Molly

"That's so sweet." I close the diary.

Alix grins. "Let's get dinner. I'm starving!"

I glance at her outfit—bathing suit, white tee, and shorts. "You wanna change first?"

"Nay," Alix says.

I'm no relationship expert or anything, but I do know a little. Alix is still figuring things out—but after our talk, I think she's starting to get it.

Day Four
Evening
Alix

Jordyn and I are sitting at our usual table up front when Doug comes by to take our order. We chat a bit and end up going with the lasagna. Right as we're talking, my cell dings. I glance at it—then freeze.

"I can't believe this!" I lean back, feeling a chill run through me.

"What's up?" Jordyn asks, pulling out her phone.

We both stare at the picture Jordyn took earlier, but now it's different. Kate used some editing app to draw a big, red X across my face. Then, she sent it to our friends—Dylan, Grace and Nikki—and they forwarded it to us with their comments.

I hold back tears as I read through a dozen messages.

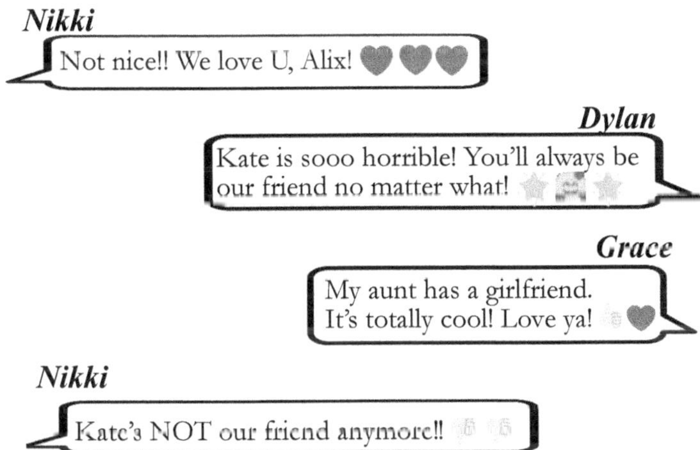

I keep staring at the X, but I can't hold it in anymore. Tears spill down my face.

Jordyn hands me a tissue.

I wipe my eyes, then glance at my phone again.

"This is beyond mean!" Jordyn says, sounding mad.

I swallow hard. "I thought Kate was my friend."

Jordyn's voice rises. "Kate's opinion shouldn't even matter. That's what you'd tell me."

Right then, Doug brings our food.

Jordyn takes a giant gulp of water. "Our real friends support you."

"I'm never going to talk to Kate again!" I say, feeling a little stronger. I glance down at more sweet texts, and they actually make me smile. I quickly text them back:

Just as I finish texting, the fancy lady shows up.

"Good evening." She looks at us closely. "I thought you looked alike. I should've known you were twins. Very cute. I could see the difference when Alix wears her baseball cap, but I don't see it tonight. How do your mom and dad tell you apart? I think I would have a hard time."

"They never mix us up." Jordyn laughs, introducing herself.

"Ridiculous question. They are your parents of course, they know," the fancy lady says with a smile. "My ring is still missing."

"I hope it's found soon," I say, feeling bad.

"You're a sweetheart," she says with a smile, patting my back. "Enjoy your dinner, girls."

"What happened?" Jordyn asks when she leaves.

"Her fancy ring went missing at the pool earlier."

"Wait, you mean that giant diamond?!"

"Yeah. She took it off to put on suntan lotion, and when she went to put it back on, it was gone."

"Yikes!" Jordyn exclaims.

I nod, and then my cell dings again. I check the text.

"Who is it?" Jordyn asks.

"Blair," I say. "Joy isn't feeling well."

"We should make her some of my famous blueberry muffins," Jordyn says, happily. "They'll cheer her up!"

"Great idea," I say. "I could use a few myself."

Jordyn takes a bite of her food. "Let's ask Dad if we can bake tomorrow morning. Oh, and we can check up on Billy too."

I nod as we finish up.

When we walk into the kitchen, everyone's busy cooking and joking around. Billy's washing fruit at the sink. We try not to get in the way until Dad notices us.

"Everything okay, girls?" Dad asks, stirring veggies in the pan.

No! Everything's not okay. But I don't want to tell him. He's at work, and I don't want to bother him. I'll just let Jordyn deal with it.

"Can Alix and I use the kitchen to make my famous blueberry muffins tomorrow morning?" Jordyn asks.

"Sounds great. Come early," Dad says, still stirring.

"Sweet," Jordyn says. I try to smile, but he's too focused to notice anyway.

"Have a good night, girls!" Dad calls as we head out.

Back at the suite, I have this sinking feeling in my stomach.

"I have an idea." Jordyn grabs the diary.

"Yeah?" I rub my forehead.

"After we bake the muffins, we should go to that candle store on Collins Ave. Remember how great-grandma Rose wrote about how candles get rid of bad energy?"

"Yeah."

"I was reading Molly's diary earlier, and she had a lot to say too," Jordyn says, showing me the page.

May - 1926

Dear Diary,

I am struggling with math class. It's not my thing. I prefer reading and writing poetry. But Rose suggested I light a candle for good energies and to invite spirits.

We went to the local candle shop where you can watch the owner make the candles. It was so interesting! There were so many kinds. Rose said it's fun to use candles to bring good vibes into your life. Different colors have different means. Since I'm bad at math, we picked a yellow one to help me focus, and it worked! I also jotted down what the other colors do:

PINK - Love, forgiveness, and friendship

BRIGHT ORANGE - Motivation, enthusiasm

POWDER BLUE - Creative inspiration

YELLOW - Concentration, focus, great for studying

BLACK - Protection, banishing negativity

RED - Courage and positive energy

GREEN - Abundance

It feels great to have candles around. Rose said after reading the Magical Powers Book that lighting them strengthens our powers. Makes sense to me!

I love my new candle and can't wait to get more.

Bye for now.

Molly

"Let's get a black one," I say, closing the diary.

"I knew you'd say that," Jordyn says, yawning as she crawls into bed.

Lying in bed, I can't stop thinking. Kate took mean to a whole new level today. There's zero excuse for what she did. I'm not telling Blair. She'll probably wonder why I was ever friends with someone like her. I feel like a fool. Blair can't ever find out!

DAY FIVE
MORNING
Jordyn

Dad's scribbling on a notepad, humming to some weird 80's song when Alix and I walk into the kitchen.

"Morning, Dad!" I say, spinning around like I'm on a dance floor.

Dad looks up and smiles. "Morning, girls! Up bright and early, I see."

"Did you get all the stuff for the muffins?" Alix asks.

"Yes, let's grab everything from the back," Dad says, leading the way.

As we follow him, I notice how shiny everything is. With the lights on and no staff around, it's like a whole new place. The big fridge has a glass door and is packed with all sorts of food. Ace's fridge back home is big, but this one's massive.

Dad hands us all the muffin ingredients, and we carry them to the front counter. "So, Alix, I heard you've got a new friend," he says, grabbing the kitchenware.

Alix blushes. "Yeah."

"When do I get to meet this mystery girl?" Dad laughs while turning on the oven.

"Uh, soon, I guess." Alix shrugs, rinsing the blueberries.

"Very exciting. Riiight!" I tease, spraying the muffin pan.

"It is," Dad says, just as Billy walks in.

I send a thought to Alix: *Act normal. Don't let Billy know we're onto him.*

I receive Alix's thought: *Got it.*

"Hey, Alix and Jordyn," Billy says, gripping the straps of his backpack.

"Hi," Alix says, and I give him a fake smile.

"What are you making?" Billy asks, acting like he actually cares.

"My famous blueberry muffins," I say, measuring flour and not falling for his act.

"Save me one." Billy laughs, heading to the back.

Yeah, right, I think. Like that's ever gonna happen!

"Girls, do you remember Grandma's cousin Silvia?" Dad asks while getting the sugar. "She lives in Florida and used to visit when you were little."

"Did she have white hair?" I ask, trying to remember.

"Yes. Her granddaughters, Kathy and Vicki, are coming to visit her from New Orleans."

"Are they our second cousins?" Alix says, looking confused.

"Technically, they're third cousins," Dad says. "Silvia figured it'd be nice for everyone to meet."

"Cool! It's important to know all our family members," I say, cracking an egg.

"Couldn't agree more. Family's what matters most," Dad says, passing Alix a spatula.

"When are they coming?" Alix asks, mixing the cream and sugar.

"New Year's Day," Dad says, glancing over my shoulder.

I turn and see Billy standing there with a list. "Here's what we need for tonight," he says to Dad.

"I have a list too. We'll hit the market soon," Dad says. "Oven's ready—those muffins should bake up real nice."

"Thanks, Dad!" we say together.

Billy waves as he takes a call and leaves.

Dad reminds us, "I need the kitchen back when I return. And

don't forget to turn off the oven."

"We'll be done," I promise.

"Have fun!" Dad calls as he heads out the door.

"Bye," Alix shouts.

Alix and I mix everything together, and soon the muffins are in the oven. We start cleaning up while we wait for them to bake when Alix suddenly yells, "Where's my bracelet?!"

"Did you leave it on the counter?" I ask, scanning the kitchen.

"I don't think so," Alix says, panicking.

We tear the place apart, then freeze and stare at the oven.

"Oh no! My bracelet's in the batter!" Alix blurts.

I grab oven mitts, pull out the pan, and dig through the gooey muffins.

"Got it!" I shout.

"Thanks, Jordyn!" Alix quickly rinses the bracelet. "Blair would've freaked if anything happened to it."

"Here, let me hook it tighter so it doesn't escape again."

"Yeah, good call."

I glance at the kitchen—total mess. Then Alix says, "We've got to make another batch before Dad gets back."

I check the clock. "No way, there's not enough time."

We lock eyes and say together, "Power time!"

Gold stars swirl around the kitchen, and BAM! The muffins are perfect, sitting on a tray.

"Awesome!" I say as we begin cleaning up.

Later, we take the muffins to Blair and Joy's room. Alix knocks, and Blair opens the door with a smile.

"These look amazing!" Blair says, taking the plate.

"Hope you and Joy like them," Alix says, just as Joy calls out a thank-you from inside.

"Feel better!" I shout back.

I'm going to hang out with Joy and finish my painting," Blair says. "Looks like it might rain."

"We're checking out the stores on Collins Avenue," Alix replies.

"I'll text you later," Blair says, leaning in to whisper something to Alix. They giggle, and I step back, feeling totally left out.

When we stop at our suite to grab our knapsacks, Grandma FaceTimes us.

"How's my favorite girls today?" Grandma asks, with her bright pink lipstick on.

"I'm good," I say, but Alix stays quiet.

"Why the long face, Alix?" Grandma asks. Sometimes, I swear she has magical powers—like she can read our minds.

"Remember Kate?" Alix mumbles.

"What'd she do?" Grandma asks.

"When she found out I like girls, she put a big red X over my face in a picture and sent it to all our friends."

"Tsk, tsk, tsk." Grandma shakes her head. "Not everyone will agree with who you like, and that's just how life is. But it's nobody's business but yours. What I don't understand is why she had to be so mean."

Alix shrugs slightly. "She's awful, Grandma!"

"Don't waste your energy staying mad at her or anyone," Grandma says calmly. "It's not worth it. Just let it go, and move forward."

Alix sighs. "I'll try."

"Okay, totally random, but—I finished my painting!" I say, hoping to lighten the mood.

"Good for you, Jordyn!" Grandma beams. "I'm so proud of you."

"Thanks! And thanks for always driving me to art class," I add with a smile.

"Of course, my darling," Grandma says, giving me a wink.

I check the time. "Grandma, we gotta run!"

"Go, go!" she laughs, blowing kisses as we click off.
We grab our knapsacks and head out.
"I really hope I can just move on from all this," Alix mutters.

Alix

As Jordyn and I are about to leave the hotel, we spot Doug in the lobby, looking gloomy with his hands shoved in his pockets, staring at the floor.

"Are you okay?" I ask, a little worried.

He looks up and suddenly starts ranting. "Billy is a snake! Last night, I was joking with him about always being late for his shifts—I wasn't even coming at him that hard. But honestly? I'm so over picking up his slack."

"I totally get that," Jordyn says, nodding.

"So, today I get a message from the manager to see him." Doug clenches his cell. "And guess what? He fired me!"

"That's awful!" I say, shocked.

"I didn't even get a chance to explain," he says, his voice a little shaky. "I'm taking classes at the university, and this job was helping me cover tuition and everything."

"I'm so sorry," Jordyn says softly.

"I didn't mean to lose it on you." Doug's phone buzzes, and he checks it. "My ride's here. I'm outta here! Take care—"

Doug rushes out, leaving us both kind of stunned.

"The uncle completely has Billy's back," I say as we start walking toward the candle store.

"We need solid proof, or no one's gonna believe us," Jordyn says, determined.

"Exactly!"

When we walk into the store, this bald guy with a name tag that says 'Luke' comes up to us.

"These are all hand-poured," he says, smiling as he gestures to the shelves full of many candles.

"Cool!" I say, glancing around at all the options.

"Each one's made with all-natural ingredients, too," Luke adds. "Let me know if you need help."

"Thanks," Jordyn replies, already scanning the shelves.

We spend the next ten minutes sniffing every black candle.

"This is it." Jordyn grabs the one with three wicks. "The scent is super strong."

"Let me smell." I lean in. "Ooh, it's like orange and vanilla. This one's perfect."

"If you've got drama going on, this will help clear out all that bad energy," Luke says as he wraps it in tissue paper.

"That's exactly what I need," I say, taking the bag. "Thanks!"

I push open the door, and the air outside is hot and sticky, and the sun's hiding. I then see Kate heading our way, and my stomach drops.

"Kate's coming," I say. Jordyn looks up fast.

"Let's cross the street," she says. "Grandma told us not to waste our energy being mad—but she didn't say we had to talk to her."

The street's full of people and cars. There's no way we can cross.

"We've got to use our powers," I say. "The freeze-in-time one."

"Yes." Jordyn grins.

We do our thing, and in seconds, everything and everyone around us is frozen. It's so quiet and still. We zig-zag through the *frozen* cars and make it across the street. From a distance, I spot Kate, frozen in place. Too bad she can't stay like that forever. But I don't want to be mean, even if she is. I push the negative thoughts away as Jordyn and I un-freeze everything.

"Wow!" Jordyn exclaims. "This is our best power yet!"

"Agreed!" I'm so glad we have these powers. "Do you think she saw us?"

"Whatever," Jordyn says, brushing it off as we walk a few more blocks.

We then stop in front of a famous bakery.

"Alix, let's go in."

I follow Jordyn inside and it's packed. We get separated in the crowd, and I shout, "Do you want a chocolate one?"

"I can't hear you!" Jordyn yells back.

Suddenly, I hear her thoughts: *I figured this would be easier than shouting. Pause. Should we use the freeze-power again? This can take forever.*

Let's not get carried away! I send back.

Pleeeeeese? she begs.

No! I send back firmly.

I finally squeeze my way to the counter and order two chocolate cupcakes, raising them above my head so Jordyn can see. She gives me a thumbs-up. I pay and shove the box in my bag with the candle and try to get out. The crowd is insane. And just my luck, I end up bumping right into Kate. We're stuck, face to face. My whole-body tenses, and all my anger comes rushing back.

"Why are you so mean to me?!" I shout, holding onto my bag so tight my fingers hurt. Before she can answer, the crowd pushes me away.

Finally, I make it outside and gasp for air. A few seconds later, Jordyn rushes out.

"I just ran into Kate!" I blurt out, still fuming.

"Just now?" Jordyn asks.

"Yes! I asked her why she's so mean, but then we got split up."

"We can run, but we can't hide!"

Day Five
Early Evening
Jordyn

lix and I rush into the hotel just as it begins to rain, and the wind goes wild. The second I get inside the suite; I dart to the patio and grab my painting. *Phew!*

"It's awesome!" Alix says, staring at it. "Not even a drop of rain got on it."

"Good thing I stuck it under the awning."

Alix pulls out the cupcake box, puts it on the table, and places the candle right next to it. She then checks her cell.

"Blair invited me to come over for a while," she says.

"Cool."

"We'll have the cupcakes when I get back," Alix says, halfway out the door. "Wait for me to light the candle."

"Totally!" I yell.

I'm admiring my painting, imagining how amazing it'll feel when I win, when Jackson FaceTimes me.

"Hey, what's up?" Jackson asks, looking extra cute today in his Rangers beanie. "Is that the painting you're working on?"

"Yep." I didn't even realize he could see it in the background.

"It looks great."

"Thanks," I say, grinning. "It's for the art contest in two days."

"You're gonna crush it!" He smiles.

"I've never done this before."

"Well, there's a first time for everything," Jackson says with a little laugh.

I nod. "How are the tryouts going?"

"I made it past the first cuts."

"That's awesome!" I'm not even a little surprised.

He grins.

"Did you hear? Kate's in Miami, staying with her Nana—literally right down the block from our hotel."

Jackson shakes his head. "I didn't know. Vaughn's off skiing in Maine with his family. Haven't heard from him."

"So, I guess you don't know what happened."

"No. What's up?" Jackson looks at me, waiting.

"Alix is hanging out with Blair, this girl she met at the pool. I guess they're kind of going out."

"Cool."

"Well, Kate doesn't think so. She put an X over Alix's face on a picture and sent it to all our friends," I say.

"That's messed up!"

"Right!"

"I'm back," Alix announces, strolling in.

I turn to her, holding up a hand and mouthing, "It's Jackson. One sec."

Then I look back at him. "Alix just got here."

"Hi Jackson!" Alix yells.

I glare at her as she hums to herself.

"Hey!" he calls out. "I'll let you go."

"Wish you were here!"

"Me too." Jackson grins. "Have fun with your sis."

I wave goodbye and click off.

"I thought you were staying longer."

"Blair and Joy ordered in room service. Their mom wanted an early dinner so they could watch a movie while their dad works." Alix pulls a purple paper butterfly from her knapsack. "And Joy's feeling way better."

"Must've been our muffins." I laugh. "Where'd you get that?"

"Blair taught me origami," Alix says, handing it to me. "It's part of her Japanese culture."

"It's so pretty," I say. "What does origami mean?"

"I asked Blair the same thing." Alix giggles. "It's the art of folding paper into shapes."

"Ooooh, look at you getting all creative!" I tease, placing the butterfly on the table.

Then Grandma FaceTimes us.

"Hi!" I dash over to sit next to Alix.

"How's everyone doing?" Grandma asks, wearing another one of her cardigans.

"I saw Kate today at the bakery shop," Alix says, shifting around.

"And?" Grandma asks.

"It was so crowded in there. I was trying to leave when we ran right into each other," Alix says.

"And?" Grandma says, waiting for more.

"I yelled at her, but then we got split up, so she never even had a chance to say anything," Alix huffs. "Who knows if she would've anyway?"

Grandma's voice turns all serious. "Alix, sweetheart. And Jordyn, I think—"

Alix cuts her off. "I'm never forgetting what she did!"

"Hold on a sec." We both nod. "I want you to let it go. We talked about this—dwelling on it is a waste of time. Don't keep replaying it."

"I'll try not to," Alix says softly.

"I know it's tough, but you need to make the effort. I've seen people drive themselves crazy because they couldn't let go of bad experiences. Don't let Kate get to you." Grandma stretches her neck and looks behind me. "Is that a candle on the table?"

"Yeah," I say.

"Good." Grandma smiles. "Light the candle and let all the

bad energy go."

"Are you sure I can't say anything to Kate?" I challenge.

"Jordyn, take my advice," Grandma says firmly.

"Okaaay!" Grandma's right.

"Love my twinnies!" Grandma waves goodbye.

"Bye, love you too!" we both say together as I tap off.

"Alix let's light the candle with our powers," I say after searching everywhere for something to light it with and finding nothing.

"Good idea," Alix says. "Focus and don't rush—we don't want to burn the hotel down."

We channel our powers, and tiny gold stars float around the candle, filling the room with a warm glow. It smells amazing too.

Alix stares at the flickering flame. "I'm done thinking about Kate!"

She squeezes her eyes shut, focusing hard.

"Goodbye, negativity!" I cheer, sneaking a glance at her.

She opens her eyes and grins. "I'm moving on!"

"Yes!" I say. "Let's celebrate with cupcakes."

"Dessert before dinner?" Alix asks.

"Why not!"

Alix opens the box, grabs a cupcake, and takes a huge bite. "Wow—this is epic!"

I grab one too and take a big bite. "This. Is. So. Good!"

Then, out of nowhere, I start jumping on my bed.

"C'mon, Alix!" I shout.

She laughs and jumps on hers too. We're having a blast when Dad suddenly bursts in and drops a bag on the table.

"Dad!" I shout, quickly stopping and getting off the bed as Alix follows.

"Everything okay?" Alix asks, catching her breath.

"Things aren't good." Dad's hair is a mess, and he starts

pacing. "The hotel manager, Axel, came in today."

"Alix and I met him the other night," I say.

"He's a real tough guy, that Axel. And he told the kitchen staff someone's been stealing from the safe. He thinks it's an inside job."

Alix and I immediately lock eyes.

"Axel said if no one confesses, he'll have to get the police involved." Dad keeps pacing. "This could turn into a big investigation and a lot of people could lose their jobs. Even me."

"Dad, you have nothing to worry about," Alix says. "You didn't do anything!"

"I know." He sighs. "But when people get scared, they start blaming others—even if they're innocent."

"This is awful!" I say.

"My whole reputation's at risk if someone accuses me for something I didn't even do," Dad says. "I'm finally making a name for myself here. If people think I was involved, I'll never get asked back."

Our jaws drop.

"I brought some shrimp and pasta." Dad finally stops pacing and takes out the food boxes. "I don't know what's going to happen. Heck, I just don't know…" His voice trails off as he walks out.

"Axel looks like the kind of guy who'd crush anyone. I mean, look what he did to poor Doug," I say. "We have to prove Billy's the thief!"

"And fast!" Alix adds. "Dad's whole career is on the line!"

Jordyn

The next morning, Alix and I are standing outside of Kehler's, and I yank on the door handle. "It's locked. Again."

"Billy better be here."

"We have to catch him," I say, determined. "Power time!"

We focus and concentrate, and —click—the door unlocks. We sneak in like total spies…until—WHAM! Alix slams right into a table.

"OW," she whisper-yells, clutching her leg.

I whip around. "Shh!" I whisper. "Real smooth."

She glares at me. "Sorry! That table came out of nowhere."

"Come on," I say softly.

We tip toe toward the kitchen. The lights are on, and the oven's running. There's a pot of water boiling on the stove. At the back, near the safe, Billy's hunched over, stuffing cash into his backpack.

"Perfect timing!" Alix says softly.

My heart's pounding like crazy. "Let's do this," I whisper back. "Get your phone ready to take a pic when we freeze him."

Alix gives me the thumbs-up. We use our freeze-in-time power, and stars start swirling around the kitchen.

"Uh-oh!" I whisper-shout. The lights flicker, and the stove and oven teeter on and off, making weird noises. And Billy isn't frozen.

He spins around, scanning the kitchen.

"Alix! It didn't work!" I whisper. "Get down! We can't let him see us."

Alix ducks behind a counter and I hide behind a big column.

Alix sends me her thought. *We have to use our powers to fix this.*

I send one back: *We're gonna get caught!*

Alix's thought: *Chill out!! Concentrate and don't rush.*

We do it again, taking our time. The lights stop flickering, and everything goes back to normal.

We crawl out of the restaurant. Once we're outside, we jump to our feet and run into the lobby bathroom. I check under every stall to make sure we're alone.

"Alix. I can't believe we messed up!" I say. "Total fail!"

"I know!" She rubs her forehead.

"Now what?" I wash my hands, which are gross after all the crawling.

"We'll just have to try again," she says, washing her hands too. Then her eyes suddenly widen. "Wait. I just thought of something."

"What?" Alix looks like she's seen a ghost.

"We forgot to lock the door when we left," she says, panicking. "We have to cover our tracks!"

"Oooh no!"

We look at each other and sprint back to Kehler's.

Alix takes a deep breath. "Focus! We can't mess up again!"

We concentrate, and little yellow stars float around the door. I check it—it's locked.

"Phew! That was way too close."

"Let's get out of here," Alix says as we speed-walk back to our suite, where we run into Dad.

"Good morning. Why are you up so early?" Dad asks, looking super tired with his shirt untucked.

"Umm—" I glance at Alix.

"We needed to use the computer in the lobby," Alix says, trying to sound normal. "Jordyn's art contest is tomorrow, so we were checking the time."

"Yeah, the time," I add.

"When is it?" Dad asks.

I try to picture the flyer in my head. Think fast. "Noon!" I blurt out, surprised I remembered.

"I saw the painting the other night. I should've told you it looks beautiful, but I've been so wrapped up in everything," Dad says. "No one knows who the thief is. It's stressful in the kitchen."

"I hope they catch the crook soon," Alix says.

"Me too." Dad sighs. "I have to get ready for the breakfast crowd. See you later. And I do plan on attending the contest."

Dad walks away, and I feel bad for lying. But it was just a little white lie. We're trying to catch Billy, which would totally help him.

After Alix and I change into our swimsuits, I check the mini fridge while Alix reads a text.

"Do you want to go to the beach today?" she asks me.

"No pool?"

"Blair's going to the beach, and she says it's really fun," Alix says, typing away. "It's right across the street."

"Yeah, I love riding the waves."

"Cool," Alix mumbles, still typing.

They're always texting like they've got a million secrets. I mean, I'm glad Alix is happy, but I seriously don't get what she sees in Blair. There's gotta be something, I guess. I grab a slice of cheese and slam the fridge shut.

It's still early, so I have time to read Molly's diary. I find a really interesting entry:

June - 1926

Dear Diary,

People must understand that even though identical twins look the same, they are different people. I know I look like Rose, but sometimes I wish friends would take the time to get to know me. We have different personalities.

I had a little issue with a boy I liked. He kept mixing up Rose and me. It changed when I started wearing my hair in braids so he wouldn't get us confused. It worked. We're now studying together, and he walks me home from school. He really knows me. I don't even have to wear my braids anymore.

I have to help with dinner now.

Bye for now.

Molly

"Alix, did Blair ever confuse you with me?"

"No! She completely saw the differences right away," Alix responds. "Why?"

"I just read this entry." I hand it to her.

"Did Jackson ever have trouble telling us apart?" Alix asks after reading.

"Not at all. We were always in class together—he knows me."

Alix grins. "Plus, the outfits help. I mean, everyone knows I'm the plain one."

I laugh, and then we get a text—group chat. We join in.

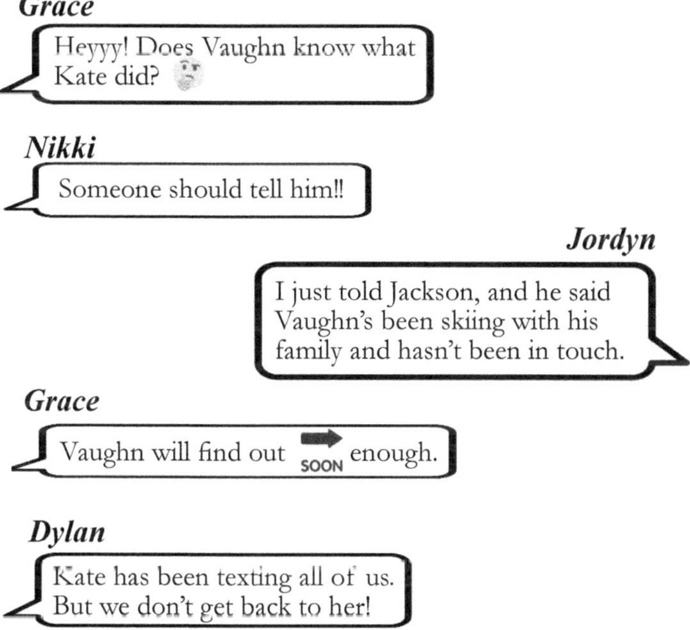

"We've moved on, but they can do whatever feels right," Alix says. "It's not up to me to decide."

"Couldn't agree more!" I say, nodding.

Grace

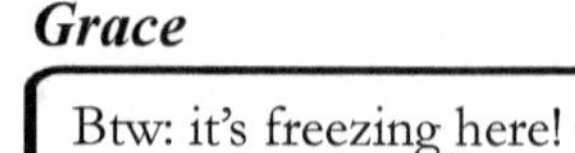

Nikki

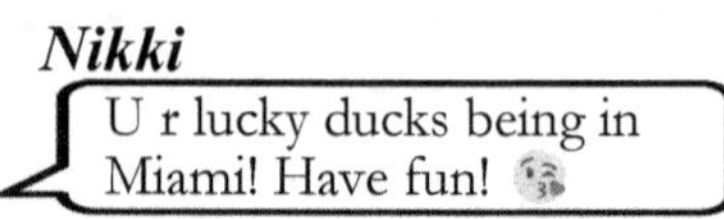

Alix

"Do you think Vaughn will break up with Kate when he finds out?" I ask, nudging Alix.

She just gives this tiny shrug, like she doesn't want to think about it.

I sigh. Whatever. I just really hope we catch Billy. Dad's worked way too hard for this—it's just not fair.

I then glance at my painting. The contest's tomorrow, and I'm kind of freaking out—but really excited. I have to win. There's no way I'm losing this!

Day Six
Afternoon
Alix

I spread my towel on the sand while Jordyn follows. The sun feels amazing, and the ocean looks sparkly. Blair and Joy show up with sandwiches and fruit. Waves crash in a soothing rhythm—it's the perfect beach day. Just as the cabana boy finishes setting up our umbrella, the fancy lady strolls by.

"I'm still looking for my ring," she says. "I'm not giving up yet."

"I hope you find it!" I shout as she continues walking.

"My app's going live on New Year's Day," Blair says, jangling her bracelets. "I can't wait."

"That's so cool!" I say.

"How are you promoting it?" Jordyn asks, sounding a bit challenging.

"I've got a huge following on Insta and TikTok," Blair says, lowering her sunglasses giving Jordyn a look. "I'll make sure all my followers know."

"I'm going in the ocean," Joy suddenly announces, hopping up from her blanket.

"I'll come with you," Jordyn says, brushing Blair off.

They run into the water, leaving Blair and me alone.

"There's a party at Kehler's tomorrow for New Year's Eve," Blair says. "Joy and I are going—you should come! There's going to be dancing too."

The sun makes her straight black hair shine, and her skin

looks golden- brown. She's perfect. I can't stop staring.

"I'm definitely coming, and so is Jordyn, but dancing?" I bite my lip. "I'm not sure about that."

"I love dancing! I've posted so many clips on TikTok," Blair says, grabbing my cell to show me.

"Wow! Is there anything you can't do?"

Blair laughs, then her phone rings and she answers it.

I spend a few minutes brushing the sand off my towel, then check my phone. The picture of me with the red X over my face pops up. Be strong, I tell myself. I'm not letting this get to me.

"Allllix! Come in!" I look up—Jordyn and Joy are splashing around in the ocean.

Blair's still talking. I give her a quick wave to say I'm heading in, toss my phone down, and take off. The sand's burning hot, so I dash into the water—and it feels amazing. We're all having fun when Jordyn goes out a bit deeper and starts riding the waves.

"Whoopee!" she shouts.

Joy follows, yelling, "Woo-hoo!"

I dive in too, catching a wave. It's so exhilarating—I don't have a care in the world. "Yahoo!"

After a while, I ride my last wave back to shore. I grab my towel and start drying off, but then I see Blair staring at my phone. My stomach drops. I forgot to close it. I'm so embarrassed, I want to run back into the ocean and never come out. Instead, I sit down slowly and dig my feet into the sand.

"Why didn't you tell me?" Blair asks, her voice soft.

"I don't know," I say, rubbing my forehead. "I guess I thought you'd judge me for having such awful friends."

Blair's eyes go wide. "What? I'd never do that."

"I'm over it," I say quickly. "But I'm not talking to her ever again."

Blair nods. "Hey, you didn't do anything wrong. Kate's the

one out of line. I'm really sorry she hurt you."

"That means a lot to me," I say, looking at her. Suddenly, I feel a warm glow inside me.

Blair reaches over and squeezes my hand.

I squeeze hers back—tight.

Suddenly, I hear a scream. "Mommyeeee!"

A little girl with pigtails is standing by the shore, surrounded by jellyfish, crying her eyes out. We all run over.

I send my thoughts to Jordyn: *Get them away from her!*

Jordyn's thoughts come back: *So scary! Let's do this!*

We swap ideas and agree on a plan. Stars float around the jellyfish, and in seconds, they're gone.

The girl's mom rushes over, plastic shovel and pail in hand, and scoops her up. "What happened?"

"She got scared by all the jellyfish," Jordyn replies. "But they're gone now."

The mom wipes her daughter's tears, then looks at us. "Thank you so much for helping her."

"You're welcome!" I say with a smile, watching them head back to their chairs.

"That was cool how the jellyfish just swam away when we showed up. Maybe they didn't like my perfume," Blair jokes, and we both giggle.

Jordyn sends me her thought: *Terrific job!*

I flash her a thumbs-up as we head back to our towels and start eating lunch.

"Pass the blueberries, pleeeeaase!" Joy sings in a sing-song voice.

Blair takes a few and passes over the container. "So, I heard sixty kids entered Kennedy's Art Contest this year. Last year it was only forty," she says, popping a berry in her mouth.

Jordyn shrugs and grabs a sandwich. "I'm not worried."

Blair leans in. "Kids are coming from all over. It's really

competitive," she says seriously. "This is a whole new level."

Jordyn fidgets a little.

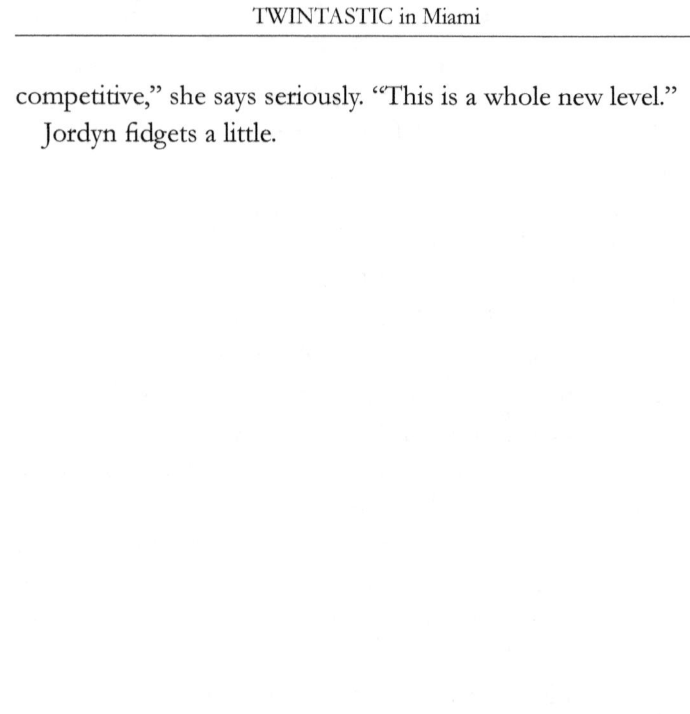

DAY SIX
EVENING
Jordyn

Alix is putting stuff away while I'm on the bed, reading the diary. When I turn the page, there's a newspaper article tucked inside. I unfold it. "Hey, Alix, check this out."

Gazette News

April – 1926

Once again, twins Molly and Rose Davis are giving back to the community. The girls volunteer weekly at the local hospital, reading to the sick children. Molly said, "It's a privilege to read to these young kids. They love hearing the poems I have written, and afterwards, they're all smiles. It's the least I can do for them." Rose reads classics like The Little Prince, The Wizard of Oz, and Peter Pan to the youngsters, which she also finds very rewarding. Thanks to the altruistic twins for bringing joy to the children!

"Whether they use their magical powers or not, Molly and Rose were always helping people," Alix says. "They were great."

"When we get home, we should volunteer somewhere, too."

"Yeah, definitely!" Alix nods as my phone pings. I glance down—Jackson texted me. I type back fast before looking up again.

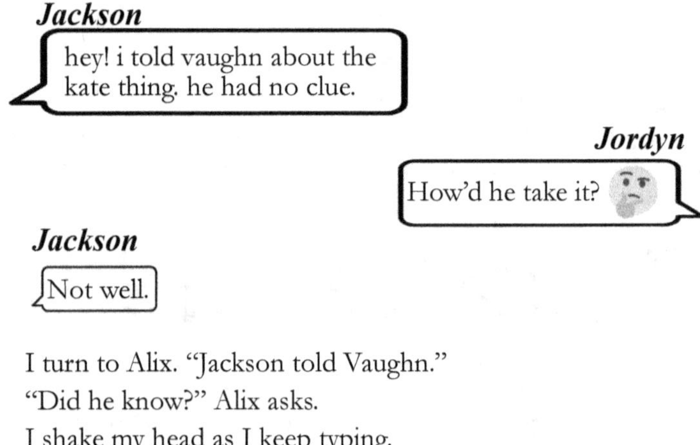

I turn to Alix. "Jackson told Vaughn."

"Did he know?" Alix asks.

I shake my head as I keep typing.

I set my cell down. "Think Vaughn will stop talking to Kate after what she did?"

Alix rolls her eyes. "Not this again. Who even cares?" she says. "Ready for the contest?"

"You bet!"

"Let's order room service and watch a movie," Alix says, flopping on her bed.

"Now that's a great idea!" I say, grinning.

I can't wait for the art contest tomorrow. I don't even mention how competitive Blair is with me—but Alix already knows. She'll probably cheer for both of us, and that's fine. Still, let's be real—I'm winning this contest. Blair acts like she's already has it in the bag. Good luck with that.

DAY SEVEN
MORNING/AFTERNOON
Jordyn

lix is already up when I get a text from Jackson wishing me good luck with the art contest. He's the best! Then, Mom and Grandma start texting too—oops, I totally forgot to tell them it's today. Dad must've told them. I jump out of bed, snap a quick pic of my painting, and send it with a red heart.

"Jordyn! We need to check out the kitchen and grab breakfast!" Alix shouts. She's already dressed and way too full of energy for this early.

"Now?"

"Yes!" Alix huffs.

I brush my teeth, throw on my light blue sundress, and search for my slides.

"Hurry up!" Alix grumbles by the door, her arms crossed. "They're under the bed."

"Okay, okay." I slip them on, and we race down the hall to Kehler's. I push open the door. "Keep watch."

We weave through the restaurant, dodging people munching on breakfast, and slip into the kitchen. No sign of Billy. Seriously? He's like a ghost—always disappearing right when we need to catch him.

"Jordyn, it's your big day!" Dad says, his eyes looking tired. He stretches his arms, then pats the counter. "Let me whip up a nice breakfast. You can eat in here."

"Are you sure?" Alix asks, knowing how swamped he is.

"There's nothing I won't do for my daughters." Dad grabs a pan and starts cooking.

"Thanks, Dad!" we say at the same time.

I send a thought to Alix: *Can you believe Billy's not here.*

She shoots me one back: *How are we ever going to catch him?*

I shrug: *No clue.*

She sends one more: *We'll just have to keep on trying. Maybe tonight!*

I nod as Dad sets plates in front of us—sunny-side-up eggs with toast.

"Yum!" I say.

We're digging in when Alix gets a text from Blair. "Can we stop by and pick her up before the contest? She needs help carrying her painting?"

"No way!" The last thing I need is to deal with Blair before my big moment.

"Please, Jordyn!" Alix says.

"Can't she ask Joy?" I say, taking a bite out of toast.

"Joy's getting her hair cut with their mom, and they'll meet Blair at the contest. Her dad's busy too," Alix explains, giving me a pleading look.

I sigh. "Fine. I guess we can."

"Thanks!" Alix grins, finishing her eggs.

I check the time. "We better get going."

"Thanks for the awesome breakfast!" Alix yells as we leave the kitchen.

"See you later, girls!" Dad calls after us.

I get my painting and cover it with a navy sheet I found in the closet. Nothing can happen to it. I start imagining my pic on every art site, looking amazing. My cheeks hurt just thinking about all the smiling I'll do. Mom, Dad, and Grandma will be so proud.

Outside Blair's room, Alix elbows me. "Jordyn, we're here."

I leave my painting in the hallway as Alix knocks. Blair opens the door, standing next to her artwork like she's already won.

I check out her painting. It's a lake with Santa fishing in a rowboat. The water's kind of muddy, the trees are just—there, and the boat looks old. I mean, I would've used brighter colors, but whatever. It's okay, I guess. She's definitely not on my level. Nothing to stress about.

"Interesting choices," I say, trying to sound nice.

"Your painting's so good! Do you have something to cover it?" Alix asks Blair. "I wouldn't want anything to happen to it."

"The weather's perfect," Blair says, waving off the idea.

Alix and Blair carry her painting while I hold mine. As we get in the elevator, Blair keeps sneaking peeks at mine. Good thing I wrapped it super tight with the sheet.

Out of nowhere, a waiter rolls in with this giant chocolate cake on a cart, and I get totally squished against the wall. Then—ding! —the elevator stops again, and out of nowhere, a basketball comes flying in, and—smack! —right into the cake. Frosting and chocolate explode everywhere, including all over Blair's painting. Total. Disaster.

"My painting!!" Blair screams. "It's ruined!"

A kid dashes in, grabs his ball, and leaves, shouting, "Whoa! Sorreeey!"

The waiter, now covered in chocolate, wipes his face with a handkerchief.

Blair looks like she's about to cry. Her yellow dress is a mess, too. Alix just has a bit of frosting on her arm, and me? Completely spotless.

When we reach the lobby, Blair slumps into a chair, looking totally crushed. Alix holds her wrecked painting.

"I can't believe this!" Blair sobs. "I'm doomed!"

I stand there, not sure what to say, while Alix jumps in. "Blair, go change. I'll fix this."

"What? It's ruined!" Blair cries, hiding her face.

Alix hands her a tissue. "Trust me, okay?"

Blair sniffles, wipes her eyes, and drags herself toward the elevator.

As soon as she's gone, Alix turns to me, her voice serious. "Jordyn. We have to use our powers."

"Are you for real?" I can't believe she'd even ask me that. She knows Blair has been super rude to me. I feel bad, sure, but not that bad. If the situation were reversed, Blair wouldn't lift a finger.

"Be nice," Alix says, giving me the look.

"Try the handkerchief like the waiter," I suggest.

"Jordyn, that's not going to work. And we're out of time." Alix wipes frosting off her arm.

I groan. "So, you want me to help your girlfriend even though she's never been nice to me?"

"Well—you haven't exactly been sweet to her either," Alix shoots back.

"Fair," I say, glancing down.

"Please, Jordyn. Help me out here?"

I look at Blair's ruined painting, then over at Alix. I know what I have to do. "Fine. I'm only doing this for you. Cause you're my twin."

"Thanks! You're the best twin!" Alix beams.

We concentrate: *Clean the painting.*

Tiny yellow stars swirl around it, and a few seconds later—it's completely spotless.

Blair comes back, her eyes still red and puffy from crying— but the second she sees the painting, her whole face lights up. "It's perfect!"

"Jordyn and I fixed it," Alix says, practically glowing.

Blair turns to her. "How'd you even do this?" Then she

throws her arms around Alix. "Thank you!"

"The chocolate came off easily. It looked worse than it was." Alix shrugs like it's no big deal.

Then—before I can react—Blair hugs me. "Thanks!"

I freeze, then slowly hug her back. "No prob," I mumble as we pull apart.

Alix checks the time. "C'mon! We can't be late!"

Blair giggles as she and Alix carry her painting, while I lug mine, sweating the whole way to the contest. Okay, maybe Blair was right to ask Alix for help—this painting is way heavier than I thought. And maybe—Blair isn't so bad after all.

We set into the grand gallery, which is packed with kids and their paintings. I hand my papers to a lady with a tight bun, and she leads me to my spot. Blair's station is further down, and Alix walks around, checking everything out.

Then I see someone who looks kind of familiar—a tall guy wearing leather bracelets, a silver chain, and with wavy light brown hair. He's got on a black tee and faded jeans, and a bunch of people with tablets are following him.

My heart skips a beat. Oh. My. God.

It's Kennedy. THE Kennedy. I recognize him from all the photos I saw on Google. Someone calls his name, and he turns around. His assistant hands him a bottled water like it's a red-carpet moment or something.

The whole gallery's buzzing. Joy comes in with her fresh haircut and her mom. A few minutes later, Dad shows up, finds Alix, and they start wandering around together.

Alix's thoughts pop into my head: *Good luck! And thanks for helping!*

I send back: *Sure thing.*

I scan the room and spot Kate at her station near a window. Her hair is perfectly straight—of course—and she's wearing pearls. I sneak a peek at her painting. It's a winter scene with pine trees and two dogs in Santa hats in the snow. The red hats pop against all the white. The dogs are ivory with black noses—super cute. I swallow hard. Kate is really good. Who knew? Now I'm sweating even more.

My thoughts are cut off when Kennedy and his crew approach me. "Thank you for sharing," he says, studying my painting while his team taps away on their tablets.

"I'm honored to be here," I manage to say, my heart racing.

Kennedy nods and smiles, and after a few minutes, everyone moves along. Phew, that wasn't too bad, but seriously, I'm sweating like crazy.

I stand there awkwardly until Dad and Alix finally show up. "Jordyn, this is terrific!" Dad says, beaming with pride.

"Thanks, Dad!" I say.

Alix nudges me. "Dad met Blair."

"She's a very talented girl," Dad adds. "Glad you two are getting along so well."

"Me too," Alix says, grinning.

"I'm sorry I can't stay longer. I have to get back to the kitchen," Dad says, rubbing his eyes.

"It's okay, I'm just really glad you came," I tell him.

"See you both tonight at the New Year's Eve party," he says with a tired smile before heading off.

"Did you see Kate?" Alix asks, peering around.

"Yeah, she's by the window," I answer. "And honestly? Her painting is good. Actually—it's great."

Alix glances at it from a distance and shrugs. "I'm not that impressed."

"You're just saying that," I mutter, sneaking another look. Kate is chatting with an elderly woman—probably her Nana.

"I'm not!" Alix shakes her head. "I'm going to check on Blair, again."

Suddenly, the announcer speaks into the mic. "Excuse me,

may I have everyone's attention?"

The crowd goes quiet.

"On behalf of Kennedy, we would like to thank all the contestants for coming out." He waves as the announcer continues, "Everyone did a fantastic job. Now for the winner—"

Okay, I got this! I tell myself, holding my breath.

"Kate Brown from Connecticut!"

Wh-what?! My head is spinning right now. I can't believe this—Kate, of all people, just won?! Kennedy's handing her a giant check for first place, and—ugh— she's doing this over-the-top victory dance. Are you kidding me?! I feel like I'm going to puke.

Alix rushes over, takes one look at me, and says, "Breathe. Just Breathe."

"I can't even!" I blurt out.

"Deep breath," she insists.

I take a deep breath and grab my painting. "Let's go!"

Just as I'm about to leave, Blair walks over, holding her painting. "You did a wonderful job. I'd love to feature you on my app."

"Wait—seriously?" I try not to sound too shocked.

"Seriously," Blair says. "It goes live on New Year's Day. Just send me your info—Alix has my email."

I glance at Alix, and she nods.

"I will!" I say, feeling a little better. I might've lost this contest, but there'll be other chances. And honestly? Meeting Kennedy was pretty awesome. Just when things start looking up, Kate walks over and stands right in front of us.

"I'm sorry, Alix!" Kate says loudly. "I really want us to be friends again."

Before Alix can say a word, Blair shouts, "We don't accept your apology!" She grabs Alix's hand, and they storm off.

I give Kate a quick glance, then head out the door behind Blair and Alix, leaving her standing there, looking kind of lost.

After a few blocks, Alix turns around. "C'mon," she yells.

"I'm getting a drink," I shout back.

She nods and keeps walking.

I duck into Dunkin for an iced tea, but of course the line is crazy long. Figures. I sigh, lean my painting against the window, and wait. While I'm stuck here, I text Jackson to tell him I lost. No reply. He's probably at soccer—at least that's what I tell myself.

Finally, I get my drink and start sipping as I head back to the hotel. I'm almost finished when a preppy boy—who looks about my age—smirks and says, "You'd look better with a tan."

Seriously? My jaw almost hits the sidewalk. That was so rude. What is wrong with people?!

I spin around. "I don't care what you think about me," I snap. "And just so we're clear—I have NO interest in you whatsoever!"

"Hey, no need to freak out!" he yells back, throwing up his hands.

I roll my eyes and keep walking, finish my drink, and toss the cup. Honestly, if I wasn't trying to be responsible with my powers, I'd turn him into a lizard in two seconds. Not sure that'd even work—just kidding. Sort of.

I dash into the suite, where Alix is washing up. I prop my painting against the wall, flop onto my bed, and kick off my slides. "Alliix! I'm back."

She rushes out of the bathroom, wiping her face with a washcloth. "Jordyn. Can you believe Kate apologized?"

"Uh-huh."

"And how cool was it that Blair stuck up for me," Alix says, grinning. "She always speaks her mind."

"No argument here," I say.

Alix sits down next to me. "Don't forget to send her your info," she adds, already shooting me a quick text with it.

I send Blair my website link. Not to brag, but it's pretty awesome—it's got all my paintings and projects from the last six months. I sign off by thanking her for including me.

Before I can even put my phone down, Grandma's FaceTiming us. I quickly answer.

"How'd it go?" Grandma asks, her eyes warm. "Your painting was spectacular! Mom loved it too."

"I lost," I tell her.

"Grandma's smile softens. "Are you okay? There'll be plenty of other contests."

"I'm fine," I say. "Really."

"In my eyes, you won just by entering," Grandma says proudly. "Not many people put themselves out there like you did."

"Thanks, Grandma," I say with a smile.

"Anything else going on?" she asks.

"Kate won," Alix chimes in. "And she apologized—she wants to be friends again."

"Good for her." Grandma leans back in her chair. "And?"

"Actually, I didn't even get a chance to say anything. Blair's the one who told her what she could do with her apology, and then we all took off," Alix explains, crossing her arms.

Grandma tilts her head and clasps her hands together like she's thinking something over.

"What do you think?" Alix asks. "I'm basically over it, but I'm not sure I want to be her friend again."

I nod in agreement.

Grandma gives us one of her wise looks. "Girls, I think I'll leave this up to your good judgment."

Alix and I exchange glances.

Grandma checks her watch. "Time to go. I don't want to keep

the ladies waiting for the card games. Then it's off to dinner, and I'll help mom at the restaurant after. Have fun, my darlings! Happy New Year!"

"Happy New Year, Grandma!" we say.

"And tell Mom too!" Alix adds.

"I will." Grandma blows us kisses and taps off.

Alix glances at her cell. "I just got a flood of apology texts from Kate."

"Maybe she actually feels bad," I say. "Like, she knows she messed up."

Alix rubs her forehead. "Yeah…I'll have to think about this some more."

I glance at my phone, secretly hoping there's a message from Jackson. Nope. Still nothing.

"Weird," I mumble.

"What's weird?" Alix asks.

"Jackson still hasn't texted back."

"And I thought I was the needy one," Alix says jokingly.

"Hey, you know what?" I say, standing up. "Blair's actually pretty cool."

Alix's face lights up with a big smile.

"C'mon!" I shout, grabbing a pillow and tossing it at her. "We've got a party to get ready for!"

Day Seven
New Year's Eve
Alix

When Jordyn and I walk into Kehler's, it looks different. The music's blasting, there's a dance floor, and silver balloons are everywhere. There's a buffet with all this fancy food by the windows. I look around for Blair, but it's so crowded I can't find her.

Just when I start feeling nervous, Blair sneaks up behind and puts her arm around my shoulder. She smells like strawberries, and it instantly makes me feel better.

"Hey!" I say, happily.

"This place looks awesome," Blair says, her eyes sparkling. "And so are you."

I giggle as Joy and Jordyn exchange greetings.

"Let's all dance!" Blair grabs my hand, and I love how she doesn't even care what anyone thinks. If it weren't for her, I'd probably be sitting in the corner. But with Blair, I feel like I can be myself. And she makes me feel special.

We're about to hit the dance floor when Jackson shows up.

"You're here!" Jordyn shouts, jumping up and down like she just won the lottery.

"This rocks!" Jackson yells, spinning around to take it all in. "Uncle Charlie came home early! And your painting was awesome."

Jordyn beams and gives him a big hug.

"Hey, Jackson!" I shout over of the music.

Jordyn introduces him to Blair and Joy, and before I know it, everyone's dancing. Blair's doing the twist, Jackson's moonwalking like a goofball, and Jordyn's spinning around while Joy sings along to the music. I'm moving to the beat, trying not to feel too awkward—but I'm actually having fun. After a while, we grab some food and find a table as the music starts to quiet down.

I'm almost done with my chicken parm when I hear Jordyn's thoughts in my head: *Hurry up! We need to check out the kitchen and see Dad.*

Good thinking! I send back.

After a few more bites, we excuse ourselves and head over. Dad is busy as ever, giving out orders to his staff.

"Girls! Happy New Year!" he says, his scruffy face lighting up.

"Happy New Year!" we shout back.

"Once the New Year rings in, I want you two heading to bed," Dads says. "That is—if you can even stay up that late."

"Deal!" I say.

"I'm totally staying up till midnight," Jordyn insists. "Jackson's here! He surprised me."

"That's exciting," he says with a tired smile. "But don't forget, we've got a big day tomorrow. Your cousins are coming."

"Can't wait!" Jordyn says as I nod.

As we're leaving, I glance over at Billy. He's chopping vegetables like his life depends on it.

Jordyn's thoughts pop in my head again: *Check out Billy. I'm shocked he hasn't sliced his finger off yet.*

Yeah, we'll have to try another time. I send back.

Everything seems great, but I wish we could catch Billy in the act. On the way back to our table, we grab some desserts for everyone.

We're all sharing the cookies and cakes when suddenly Kate shows up.

"Alix. I want to start the New Year off right!" Kate says, looking nervous. "Please—"

Blair cuts her off before she can finish. "You only won because the dogs were adorable. And everyone knows Kennedy's a dog lover."

"I'm not here to talk about why I won," Kate says, her voice shaky. "I just want to—"

Blair interrupts again. "We don't accept—"

"Let's hear her out," Jackson says, trying to keep things calm.

"Didn't you get my texts? I'm sorry! I was being a bully!" Kate's face is pale. "I want to be friends again!"

Blair just keeps shaking her head.

"Alix, please forgive me! I regret everything." Kate stares at me as tears fill her eyes. "No one's talking to me. Not even Vaughn."

I cross my arms. "You don't have to like my friends or who I hang out with—but you didn't have to be so mean to me!" Blair grabs my hand, and I squeeze hers back.

"No one likes a bully!" Blair says, her voice sharp.

"I'm really sorry!" Kate yells so loud, I'm pretty sure the whole restaurant hears. "Nana said it's none of my business who my friends like too."

Then I hear Jordyn's thoughts in my head: *Take the high road! Just accept the apology already! Stop being the queen of stubborn!*

I start arguing with myself, but Jordyn's thought jumps back in.

Let it go and move on!

I sigh, thinking it over. Holding onto this isn't helping anything. I guess Jordyn is right. I send back a thought: *Okay!*

"I accept your apology," I say out loud, and Blair squeezes my hand.

"Great, Alix!" Kate blurts out.

"Let's all go dancing!" Jackson yells as the music kicks up

again.

We dance and laugh until our stomachs hurt. Jackson hooks his arm through Jordyn's, and she links into mine. Blair, Joy, and Kate join in too, and soon we're one big, happy circle.

"Ten, nine, eight —" the crowd counts down.

I turn to Blair, grinning. "This is the best New Year's ever!"

"It is!" she yells back.

Bells clang, horns blast, and everyone screams, "Happy New Year!"

Then Kate comes over, her smile gone, looking very serious.

"I'm really happy you forgave me, Alix," she says above the noise. "Your friendship means a lot. I'm going to focus on my own stuff from now on."

"That's probably a good idea," I say.

Blair steps in, giving Kate a sharp look. "Don't be mean to Alix again."

"I won't! I promise!" Kate blurts. Then she adds, "And honestly? You two are a really cute couple!"

Blair and I laugh, and she grabs my hand as we dance to the music.

The lights, the crowd, Blair holding my hand—it all feels perfect.

****

Jordyn

"Can we talk about how great it was when Jackson surprised me?" I yawn.

"Tonight was amazing!"

"No doubt," I say.

Our group chat blows up with Happy New Year texts. I fire one back quick:

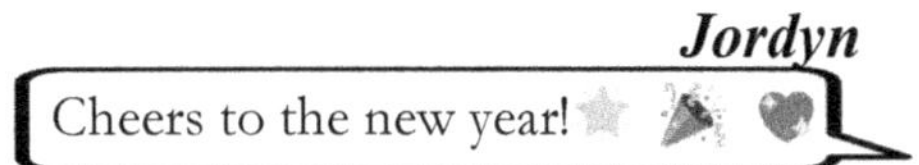

Meanwhile, Alix is typing a whole essay about Kate's apology.

"You don't have to tell them every single detail," I say, flopping onto my pillow.

"Good night, Jordyn," she says, still typing.

"One last thing—"

"Yeah?" she asks, fingers flying.

"We have to catch Billy. Time's running out," I mumble, already half-asleep.

DAY EIGHT
AFTERNOON
Jordyn

After our big night, I slept until almost noon. Now Alix and I are just hanging out by the pool, waiting to meet our cousins while I'm doodling our family tree on a napkin.

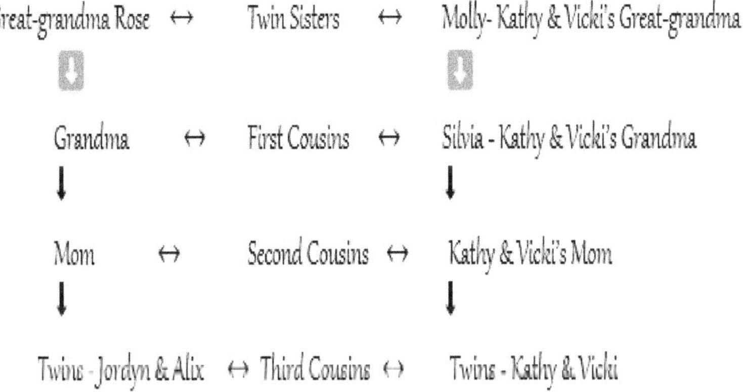

Just as I'm finishing up, Dad walks into the pool area with Silvia, Kathy and Vicki. Silvia looks just like I remembered—petite, white hair, and big hoop earrings. But Kathy and Vicki? Whoa. They're identical. People say Alix and I look alike, but these two are like the same. Olive skin, wavy brown hair to their shoulders, hazel eyes, and they're the same height too.

"Hello!" Silvia exclaims. "You've grown up so much! I remember when you were babies."

Alix and I get up from our lounge chairs, and Silvia gives us hugs. We introduce ourselves to Kathy and Vicki, and right away, I notice Vicki got a tiny freckle above her upper lip—that's how I'll tell them apart for now.

"It's so nice for all the cousins to be together." Silvia pulls up a chair and pats the seats beside her. Kathy and Vicki sit down next to her.

"I agree," Dad says, though he looks stressed. Alix overheard him tell Mom this morning that Axel is coming down hard on the staff about the theft situation. We need to catch Bill, fast.

"Jordyn!" Alix elbows me. "Kathy and Vicki like to dance."

"That's awesome!" I say, snapping back to the conversation.

"My granddaughters are excellent dancers," Silvia says proudly.

"Grandma!" Kathy blushes.

"I just tell it like I see it." Silvia squeezes their hands.

Kathy and Vicki giggle.

"Girls, Silvia and I are going to get some coffee," Dad says. "Have a fun, and we'll see you later."

"Tell Jordyn and Alix about the school play," Silvia says as they leave and blows kisses to all of us just like our grandma does.

"What play?" I ask.

"The King and I," Kathy says, scooting closer to Vicki. "We were the Siamese twin dancers. I wanted the solo dance with Anna, and Vicki tried out for the solo dance with the King."

"But our teacher made us twin dancers instead," Vicki adds. "At first, we were upset, but it ended up being perfect."

"That's cool," I say.

"My girlfriend Blair loves to dance too," Alix says.

"You have a girlfriend?" Kathy asks. "Me too!"

Alix nods. "Yeah, she'll be here soon."

"I have a boyfriend, Jackson. Maybe you'll meet him later," I add.

"Cool," Vicki says. "I've got a crush on a boy who's in my Spanish class, but I don't think he even knows I exist."

"Don't say that," Kathy says.

"It's true." Vicki laughs.

"Do you take dance lessons?" I ask.

"Yeah, we've been doing jazz since we were five, and we started hip-hop a few years ago," Vicki explains. "We love it!"

"Wow, that's incredible!" I say as the fancy lady walks by.

"Still searching," she says, waving her ringless hand.

Alix frowns. "I can't believe you still haven't found it yet."

Before she walks away, she lifts her sunglasses and notices Vicki and Kathy. "Are you also twins?" she asks.

"Yep," Kathy replies.

"How wonderful! It's a twin festival." She chuckles and then leaves.

"Isn't it great being a twin?" Kathy says, resting her arm on Vicki's shoulder.

"It's like having a built-in best friend," Vicki adds. "Have you ever switched classes or tried to trick people?"

"We never switched classes, but that would've been fun!" I nudge Alix. "If we're not in the same science class next year, let's switch—you can take my tests since you always get A's."

Alix gives me a look. "Yeah, right."

"I wouldn't do it for Vicki either," Kathy says, laughing.

Vicki grins. "Hey, being a twin means helping each other out!"

"Exactly!" I say.

Alix and Kathy both roll their eyes at the same time, and we all crack up.

"Jordyn. Remember in kindergarten—" Alix starts, but I cut her off.

"Yeah! The switcheroo game."

"Let me tell," Alix says, stopping me with her hand. I nod.

"In first grade, our class made a kid-sized Big Ben clock out of cardboard with moveable hands and Roman numerals, just like the one in London. We were learning to tell time," Alix explains. "But our teacher also used it for a game called Who's Who?"

"I never heard of it," Vicki says.

"It was a guessing game that the teacher invented," Alix continues. "Jordyn and I would hide inside Big Ben and pop out one at a time. Our classmates had to guess who was who."

"The right guess let you line up to go home early," I add. "But if you were wrong, you had to wait and try again."

"So, some kids could still be waiting!" Vicki jokes.

"Pretty much!" I say with a smile.

After chatting for a while, a staff member hands us flyers. I read mine:

Dance contest tomorrow. Sixty seconds to show the world your dance moves. Sponsored by TikTok. Winner will be featured on TikTok influencers' accounts.

Sign up at: www.miamitiktokdance.com   Behind the pool @ 2:00pm.

"This is awesome!" Kathy claps. "We're always posting our dances on Insta and TikTok."

"We should do the routine we've been working on," Vicki suggests.

"We didn't bring our dance costumes." Kathy frowns.

"We'll wear our gold shorts with tank tops," Vicki says. "If we win, we'll get so many more followers and officially be influencers!"

"Don't get ahead of yourself," Kathy says.

"A girl can dream!" Vicki grins.

"I'll follow you," I say, already opening the app.

"Same here!" Alix chimes in. "What's your user?"

We all whip out our phones, thumbs flying.

"Wanna swim?" Kathy asks, eyeing at the pool.

"Yeah, it's boiling out here," Alix says, taking off her baseball hat.

When Kathy and Vicki take off their cover-ups, I spot shiny crystal necklaces around their necks—just like the ones that Grandma gave Alix and me. But their crystals are slightly different colors. Huh. Weird.

Alix and I didn't bring ours' because Grandma was freaking out, we'd lose them. She gets overprotective sometimes.

We're splashing around in the pool when Jackson suddenly cannonballs in, drenching us.

"Hi, Jackson!" I laugh as he swims over.

"Surprise!" he grins.

You're full of surprises!"

Alix and my cousins swim up, and I wave them in. "Everyone, this is Jackson—the one I told you about."

They all say hi, and Jackson does a double take. "Wow, you two look exactly alike."

"Not exactly," Kathy says with a smirk.

"Once you know us, it's easy to tell," Vicki adds.

Jackson nods. "Yeah, I get that."

"You better," Vicki teases. "You hang out with a twin!"

Jackson shoots me a mischievous grin. "Hey—wanna race?"

"I call judge!" Alix says.

"I'm in," I say as everyone else agrees.

We race doing the butterfly stroke, and Jackson wins by a mile. Then Kathy challenges him to a freestyle race, and he wins again, but just barely.

"I was hoping you would be here." Blair suddenly appears in a sequined bathing suit, with Joy behind her.

Everybody gathers by the pool steps.

"These are my cousins, Kathy and Vicki." Alix sits on the top step.

"Hi! I'm Blair," she says, flicking her long side ponytail. "And this is Joy."

"Alix said you love dancing," Vicki says to Blair.

"I do! I've got a ton of followers on Insta and TikTok," Blair brags, pulling out her phone.

There she goes again. The more I'm around her, the more I see—she's actually kind of insecure.

"There's a dance contest," Alix says, flashing the flyer at Blair.

"I'm signing up right now," Blair declares.

"You're the best dancer ever!" Joy chimes in. "But I like singing more."

"Yeah, we noticed," Alix says, laughing.

"Hey, let me see that," Jackson calls, hopping out of the pool and snatching the flyer.

I catch his eye—he hits me with that goofy smile of his.

"Good luck!" Vicki shouts, before flipping into a somersault like it's no big deal.

Honestly, I'm just glad everyone's getting along—my cousins are actually pretty cool.

But then I glance around. No sign of Billy. Seriously? Did he take the day off or what? What I do know is this—Alix and I have to catch him. We can't let him keep stealing. Enough is enough.

Day Eight
Early Evening
Alix

I'm flipping through Molly's diary while Jordyn gets ready for our dinner with Jackson when I find a page taped in from a different year.

"Jordyn, look at this!"

January - 1924

Dearest Diary,

This week has been a mess! Last Saturday, I went to the dance with Rose. I saw Max, who I have the biggest crush on. I thought it would be a good idea to use my magical powers to make him like me. Rose agreed, so we did it. He asked me to dance and the whole night was wonderful. I was so happy. But then on Monday, he was completely different. He was quiet and not funny at all. It's like he wasn't the same *person. When we saw Max at the ice cream parlor, Rose and I used our powers to turn Max into his old self. When we finished our ice cream, Max was making me laugh again, just like he used to. I've learned that messing with people's feeling isn't a good idea.*

I'm so tired, I need go to bed!

Molly

"This is the same page we saw taped in Rose's diary a while back," Jordyn says as she finishes putting on her Chapstick. "Molly must have wanted her to have a copy."

"I get it. It's important," I say, putting the diary down.

We head over to Kehler's, where Jackson waits at the front table.

"I'm excited for dinner," Jordyn says with a big smile.

"Same," Jackson says, grinning back,

"Glad you got to meet our cousins. They're cool, right?" Jordyn says.

"Yeah—and fast swimmers!" Jackson laughs, just as his phone buzzes. He checks it. "Looks like Vaughn forgave Kate after she apologized."

Jordyn and I both nod.

"How are tryouts going?" Jordyn asks.

"Made it through another round," Jackson says, looking proud.

"That's awesome!" Jordyn beams. "When do you find out if you made the team?"

"Pretty soon. If I do, practice is every day after school next month."

"Whoa, that's serious," I say.

"Yeah, gotta put in the work," Jackson replies.

"You ready for the contest tomorrow?" Jordyn asks.

"You know it!" he says with a grin.

We all laugh—but then my phone rings. It's Blair. And she sounds…not okay. I step away.

"What's wrong?" I ask, heading into the lobby.

"I'm freaking out!" Blair says. "I've been practicing my routine, but it just feels… off."

"Keep going— you'll get it," I say, trying to sound encouraging.

Just then, I see Billy rushing out of the hotel with his backpack. I rub my forehead.

"Alix, you really think so?" Blair asks. "Alix? Hello?"

"Yeah, yeah, definitely. If anyone can pull it off, it's you."

"I'm still a little bummed about losing the art contest," Blair admits. "I can't lose the dance one too."

"You won't," I tell her. "Just have fun with it."

"Easy for you to say. I don't even remember how to just have fun anymore."

"Maybe try not stressing so much."

Blair lets out a huge sigh. "Yeah, I'll try. It's just—mom's freaking out about some drama with my dad's company, and it's driving me nuts."

"That's a lot," I say, thinking. "But tonight, just focus on you—and your routine. You've got this."

She exhales. "Okay. You're right. I'll try. Promise." Then her voice perks up. "You eating?"

"Yeah, I'm at Kehler's."

"Cool. Enjoy dinner."

"Good vibes only!" I say, then click off.

I head back to the table, still feeling bad for Blair. I want her to win so bad. But then I remember Billy. What's he even up to? Whatever it is, I'm pretty sure it's shady. We need to catch him—soon.

DAY EIGHT
LATE EVENING
Jordyn

Alix and I walk into our suite just as Grandma FaceTimes us.

"Good evening," she says, smiling.

"Why are you up so late?" I ask, a little shocked.

"I should be asking you that!" Grandma laughs. "What's new?"

"Jackson surprised me for New's Year!" I say. "He's staying with his uncle who lives nearby for a couple of days. We just had dinner with him."

"That young boy is a real gem," Grandma says, sounding really happy. "And Alix, anything new with you?"

"I accepted Kate's apology," Alix says.

"Wonderful, darling." Grandma takes a sip from her teacup. "I'm proud of my twins."

"We also met our cousins, Kathy and Vicki," I say, cheerfully. "And saw Silvia too."

"That's great news!" Grandma exclaims. "Your mom didn't tell me—she's been busy at Ace. She's still there now, closing up."

"We're going to see them again tomorrow," Alix says. "And I think they'll staying for a few days."

"Enjoy yourselves!" Grandma folds her hands together. "Sleep tight!"

"Good night, Grandma!" Alix and I say at the same time.

A few minutes later, we're both in our pajamas. I'm so excited for the dance contest tomorrow as I grab my phone.

"Check out Kathy and Vicki on TikTok," I say, holding it up.

We both stare at the screen in total silence, our mouths kind of open.

After a minute, I finally speak. "Are they seriously related to us? They're so talented. Maybe they'll become *twinfluencers*."

"This is no joke! They're amazing dancers!" Alix says, her eyes going wide. "I'm don't even know if Blair stands a chance." She grabs her cell and starts watching more videos.

"We'll see, I guess." I place my phone down, but Alix keeps scrolling. It's super annoying when she gets obsessed like this.

"Go to sleep already," I flick off the light.

"Uh-huh, good night, Jordyn," she mumbles, still glued to her phone.

Jordyn

I can't believe Alix is still sleeping. She must have been watching Kathy and Vicki's TikTok videos all night. I read through the diary for a while and find another newspaper article clipped in. I unfold it and read it.

Gazette News

August - 1926

The Charleston is all the rage.

The turnout for the Charleston Contest last night was huge. The twins, Rose and Molly Davis, won the contest for their age group. Rose and Molly couldn't be happier.

"It's a popular dance that we love," Molly said. Her twin sister added, "We never thought we'd win. We're honored to receive this award!"

Congratulations Rose and Molly!

Wow, the Roaring Twenties must've been so fun. It's awesome that Molly and Rose won the dance contest. No wonder Kathy and Vicki are so good—they probably got their moves from them. Meanwhile, Alix and I? Definitely missed out on the dance gene.

"Hey, what time is it?" Alix mumbles, yawning.

"Finally, you're up!" I glance at my phone. "It's 11:15 AM. Check this out."

I bounce out of bed, hand her the diary, and start getting dressed.

"Cool," Alix says, looking at the article. "Maybe Blair should try doing the Charleston."

I laugh. "Want to grab some iced tea with me?"

"Sure." Alix hops out of bed and checks her cell. Her face lights up.

"Really good news!" she says, texting quickly.

"What is it?" I ask.

"Blair messaged me that lots of people are downloading her app."

"Awesome! Hope they're all interested in me too," I joke, heading for the door.

"Wait a sec." Alix is still tapping away. "Blair's freaking out about the dance contest."

"Can you put your phone down for a minute?" I huff as Alix keeps typing. "Forget it—I'll just go alone."

"Do you mind?" Alix looks up for half a second, then goes right back to texting. "Now Blair's having a meltdown."

"No problem at all," I say, full-on sarcasm mode.

"And remember—extra lemon!" Alix yells as I'm already halfway down the hall.

I walk into Dunkin and Kate's right in front of me in line. Things feel normal again, but deep down I'm still not sure I can totally trust her after what she did to Alix.

"Hey, Jordyn!" Kate waves. "Want an iced tea? My treat!"

Whoa. She remembered my favorite drink. That's actually kind of sweet.

"Oh—uh—you don't have to," I say, feeling a little awkward.

"I want to," Kate says. "Does Alix want one too?"

"Yeah, that'd be great. Extra lemon for her."

Kate places the order, and while we're waiting, she gives me this random look.

"Do you try to avoid the sun?" she asks.

"What?" My whole-body tenses up.

"I mean, well, you don't have a tan," Kate says. "And we're in sunny Miami."

"Stop!" I snap, a little too loud. Of course, she tans perfectly and never burns.

Kate's eyes widen. "I was just asking."

"Look, I know I'm not all golden and glowy, okay?" I say. "I just burn super easy, so I have to be careful."

Kate shrugs. "I think your complexion's pretty, that's all."

"Oh." I blink. "Thanks!" I didn't see that coming—but it feels nice. "Actually…I like it too."

We both laugh as we grab our drinks.

"If you're free later, there's a dance contest at our hotel. It starts at two o'clock, behind the pool area," I say.

"Sounds fun," Kate says. "Any idea who's dancing?"

"Yeah," I say, nodding. "Jackson, Blair and my cousins."

"Who are your cousins?" she asks.

"They came the other day." I take a sip of my tea. "Kathy and Vicki. They're amazing!"

Kate nods as we walk toward my hotel.

"Thanks for the drinks," I say, thinking it was a really nice gesture. I guess she really is trying to be a good friend.

"Sure thing!" she says, waving as she heads off. "See ya later."

Before heading back to the suite, I stop by Kehler's to say hi to Dad. The kitchen's quiet, but I can hear the soft sounds of chopping and slicing.

Dad, who's sporting a bit of a beard, is cooking something. "What's up?" I ask. "It's so quiet in here."

"Axel let two people go," Dad says in a low voice, sprinkling some spices without even looking up.

"Wait—what? Why?"

"Someone claimed they saw them take money."

"That's awful," I say.

Dad just nods. "Grab a sandwich and take one for your sister."

I glance over at the counter—there's a whole stack of them. I take two.

"Thanks, Dad."

"We'll talk later," he says, still totally in cooking mode.

I stuff the sandwiches in my knapsack, grab the iced teas, and head out, my mind racing. This is bad. Really bad. People are throwing others under the bus just to save themselves. Dad could be next. Alix and I have to catch Billy!

"I'm baaack," I shout, walking into the suite and setting down the drinks.

Alix zooms over and grabs hers.

"I ran into Kate at Dunkin. She bought these for us."

"That was nice of her," Alix says, taking a huge sip.

"Right." I say, pulling out the sandwiches. "She's coming to the contest too."

"Cool."

"Oh—and Dad gave us these when I stopped by." I hand her one.

"How's he doing?" Alix asks.

"Things are getting worse." I unwrap my sandwich. "Two people were fired! Someone blamed them for stealing, even though we know who the real thief is."

Alix leans in, eyes serious. "We have to move fast—and *'freeze'* Billy!"

Day Nine
Afternoon
Alix

"Who keeps texting you?" Jordyn asks.

"It's Blair. She's stressed and her mom's driving her crazy," I reply.

Jordyn and I arrive at the dance contest. There are loads of people sitting on the lawn. The big stage is front and center, and a DJ is spinning hip-hop beats. We grab some seats up front. I can practically feel the excitement buzzing around.

While we're waiting, Jordyn gets a text from Jackson.

"Alix!" Jordyn stands up.

"What's up?" I ask.

"Jackson needs my hat. The one with the pink flowers."

"Why?"

"He forgot his at his uncle's place. I have to run back to the room and get it," Jordyn explains and dashes off.

"Hurry back!" I shout after her.

Just then, the fancy lady sits down in Jordyn's seat next to me.

"Hi honey," she says with a big smile. "I used to dance, but not like the dancers today."

"What kind of dancing did you do?"

"I was a ballerina." She crosses her legs gracefully. "But I love watching all kinds."

I then get messages from Blair.

Blair

I have to win. I was up all-night practicing!

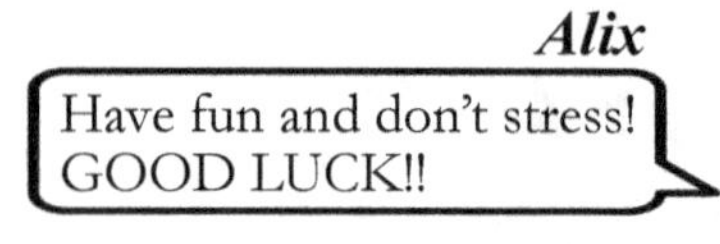

I really hope she wins. It'd mean everything to her.

Then Jordyn's thought pops into my head: *Wait—why is the fancy lady in my seat?*

I send back: *Ohhh! She just sat down, and I was so busy texting—*

More from Jordyn: *It's fine. I grabbed a seat two rows back.*

I turn, scan through the crowd, and wave at her.

The announcer walks onto the stage, mic in hand. "Get ready for the Miami Dance Contest!" The crowd cheers. "It's show time!"

The music kicks in, and the first few acts start performing.

Then it's Jackson's turn. He smiles as the music plays. He twirls Jordyn's hat on his fingers while dancing, and he's very entertaining. Jackson finishes by putting on the hat, and the crowd laughs and claps.

I peek back at Jordyn—she's got the biggest grin on her face.

A few more dancers go, including a cute girl in cowboy boots who gets a big cheer for her country dance.

Next up are Kathy and Vicki. Their performance is even better than the videos I saw last night. I look over, and the fancy lady is smiling and tapping her foot along with the beat. They rock it! The crowd goes wild.

As I'm applauding, I get more texts from Blair.

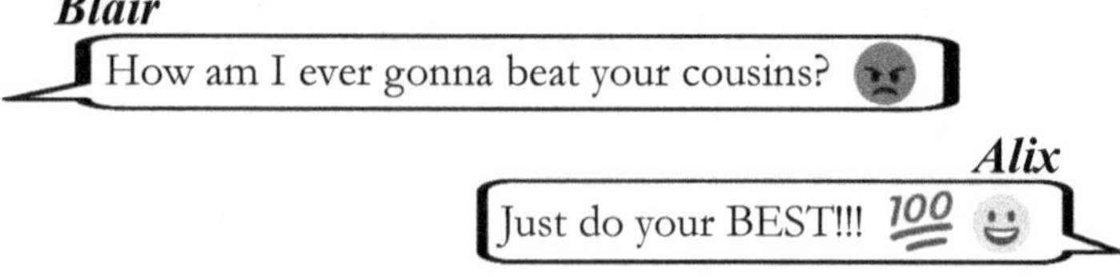

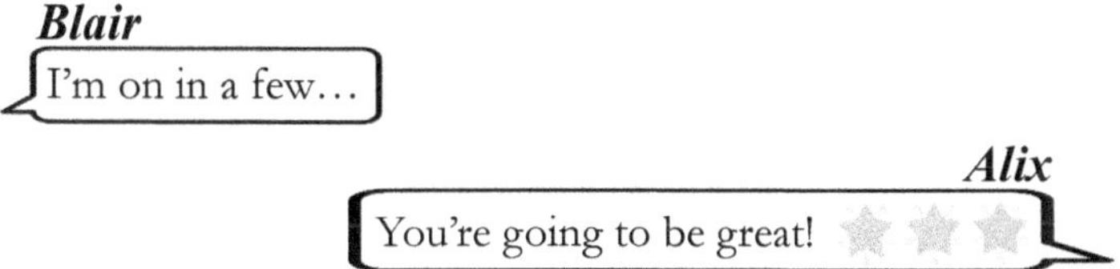

I send my thoughts to Jordyn: *Can we please use our powers for Blair? She really wants to win!*

Jordyn shoots back: *What?! Did you already forget what the diary said? We can't mess with people's emotions like that.*

I send back more thoughts: *I know. But I feel bad. Blair was upset after the art contest. She doesn't want to lose again. She practiced all night.*

Jordyn's thoughts: *Every contestant wants to win. They probably all practiced. Blair's not the only one.*

I send back another thought: *Please reconsider!*

Jordyn's thoughts: *Nope. It's cheating. Forget it.*

I send one last plea: *Please, Jordyn!*

Jordyn's thoughts: *I get it— she's your girlfriend and you want her to be happy. But cheating is still cheating! It's not fair to everyone else.*

I let out a sigh and stop responding. She's right. I shouldn't even have asked. Just because Blair wants to win doesn't mean we should interfere. The best dancer should win—fair and square.

Blair steps onto the stage looking amazing in her glittery silver outfit. She dances with this huge, confident smile, and when the song ends, she takes a big, dramatic bow. I catch her eye and wave excitedly. She walks off laughing as the crowd applauds and whistles.

When the contest ends, the announcer shouts, "And the winners are—the twins, Kathy and Vicki!" The music blasts, the crowd goes nuts, and everyone starts dancing like crazy in the aisles. The fancy lady takes my hand and spins me around, then twirls the person next to her. It's a dance party!

Blair runs over, beaming. "I took your advice and had a great time! I don't even care that I lost—your cousins were amazing."

"You were amazing too!" I yell over the music, glancing at the bracelet that she gave me. I'm going to miss her so much.

Blair's smile fades. "What's wrong?" she asks, looking worried.

"Umm…" I hesitate.

"C'mon, tell me!" she shouts.

"I'm just going to miss you!" I blurt out.

"We still got a few more days." Blair sways to the music. "But whenever you're thinking of me, I'll be thinking of you too."

"Even with all the fun stuff in the big city?"

"Yep, even with all that," she says, laughing and smiling at me.

Then my cousins come running over. "Congrats!" I shout, hugging Kathy and Vicki while Blair does the same.

Jackson makes his way around, giving everyone high fives.

Kate walks up to Blair. "You were great!" We all hug.

I pull out my phone and start recording everyone celebrating. Even Silvia joins in.

"It's for Grandma," I shout into the camera.

Everyone waves and shows off their best dance moves.

"Hi Grandma!" Jordyn yells as Jackson makes goofy faces.

"Hi, Grandma of twins!" Joy sings.

Then Blair grabs my wrist and spins me around while I'm trying to keep the camera steady. "Your granddaughter's the best!" she shouts, laughing.

That night, I can't stop watching the video. I send it to Grandma—then watch it again. And again.

Jordyn

Alix and I are almost out the door when Grandma FaceTimes us.

"What a fabulous video Alix!" Grandma exclaims. "And you both looked beautiful."

"We had our glam squad come in," I say, teasing.

Grandma laughs. "Silvia couldn't stop raving about my twinnies and how she's having a great time."

"We wish you could be here with us," Alix says.

"Maybe next time," Grandma says.

I cringe a little. I hope there'll be a next time. For all I know, Dad could get blamed for stealing and never be asked back.

"Everything all right, Jordyn?" Grandma asks.

"Yeah," I say, forcing a smile.

"Didn't you love seeing Blair on the video?" Alix jumps in.

"Yes! I'm sorry I didn't say it first." Grandma laughs. "I showed it to Mom, and she loved it as much as I did."

"Blair's amazing," Alix adds.

"Aah, she seems it." Grandma's eyes sparkle with a smile "Enjoy your day, girls!"

"Bye!" we shout together.

Grandma blows us a kiss before tapping off.

Just then, our group chat blows up, so we join in.

Dylan
When r u coming home? 🐼

Nikki

Feels like forever! Mom can't wait to make your fav Indian dessert for her fav twins!

Jordyn

Tysm! We'll be home in 2 days.

Grace

I'm upstate w/ my dad, see u guys next week. btw: we are all texting with Kate again.

Alix

All good! Can't wait to see everyone!

"I miss our friends, but I really like it here," Alix says, putting her phone away.

"It's been a great vacation," I say, nodding.

"It's not just about the vacation!" Alix blurts out. "It's everything—meeting new people, Blair, dancing, staying up late, being on our own, hanging with our cousins—"

"Alllix. I get it!" I cut in. "Let's just make the most of the time we have left. Who knows if we'll even be back?" I grab my bag and head for the door. "C'mon, I don't want to be late."

Alix gets up and drags her feet.

"Move!"

"I'm coming!" Alix shouts back.

We run down the hall and sit at the table.

"How are my super star cousins?" I ask.

"Things are happening fast," Kathy answers. "We're getting tons of followers, and some influencers want to post our dance videos."

"That's cool," Alix says.

"Kathy and Vicki." Silvia looks at them seriously. "This is exciting, but I don't want it to go to your heads. Stay humble."

Vicki and Kathy nod.

Silvia sips her coffee. "And remember to look out for each other."

"We always do," Vicki says. "Nothing's changing."

Silvia nods.

"Alix and I always look out for each other too," I add. "But trust me, there are plenty of times when she gets on my nerves."

"Same!" Alix snaps back.

Silvia smiles. "When Kathy and Vicki were babies, they always looked out for one another."

Vicki rolls her eyes. "Not this story again—"

"I have to tell this one!" Silvia says. "I used to watch the twins when their mom was at work. Kathy and Vicki shared a room, and their cribs were side by side, and if one woke up first, the first thing they'd do was look for the other."

Silvia turns to Alix and me. "One morning, Kathy woke up and couldn't see Vicki, so she started crying. I came in, and it turned out Vicki was just playing under her baby blanket. But instead of calming down, Kathy got even louder—pointing and fussing. Vicki was just under there kicking and giggling. I pulled off the blanket, picked her up, and told Kathy, 'See? Everything's perfectly fine.'"

"Whoa, that's awesome!" I say.

"We love that story, Grandma!" Kathy says with a smile. "Even if we've heard it a million times."

We're all cracking up when Billy shows up. "Ready to order?" he asks, sounding bored.

Before we can answer, Dad walks in, pushing a cart. "I got this, Billy. They're my family."

Billy shrugs and walks away.

I quickly send my thoughts to Alix: *Hope we can use our freeze-in-*

time powers today.

She shoots back: *Fingers crossed.*

"Girls, a little help here?" Dad says, unloading plates off the cart. Alix and I jump in to assist.

"We should hit the pool later," I suggest as I sit back down.

"I'm in," Vicki says, grabbing some bacon.

"Me too," Kathy chimes in, tucking her hair behind her ears.

That's when I notice her earrings. "Wait, your ears are pierced?"

"Yeah." Kathy shrugs, piling pancakes onto her plate. "What's the big deal?"

"I got two." Vicki shows off her earrings—a gold heart and a half-moon in each ear.

"I wasn't allowed," I say, frowning.

"I never wanted to get mine done. I'm not really into jewelry unless it's a gift," Alix says, showing off her bracelet. "It's from Blair."

"Beautiful," Kathy says.

"For a while that's how most of our friends told us apart," Vicki says. "I'd always show off my double pierced ears."

Another twin trick—but after spending time with them, I can totally tell who's who now.

"Yeah, it definitely helped," Kathy adds with a laugh.

I nudge Dad. "So—maybe now you'll finally let me get my ears pierced? You know, for the sake of twin identity."

Dad chuckles. "I don't think I ever had a trouble telling you two apart."

Silvia laughs too.

DAY TEN
EARLY AFTERNOON
Alix

Jordyn and I are in the gift shop looking to buy something nice for Mom and Grandma. I've got some money saved up from tutoring my friends from back home. I'm wandering around when Jordyn calls me.

"Check this out." She holds up a light green tee shirt with palm trees on it. "It says 'Miami, Florida' at the bottom."

"It's perfect!" I say. "Let's get two in medium."

We look around but can only find one. I spot a salesgirl who's busy helping a cranky guy.

"How can I help you?" the salesgirl asks cheerfully, her ponytail bouncing as she turns to us.

"Do you have another one of these?" I hold up the tee shirt. "It's a medium."

"Let's check the stock room," she says, motioning us to follow her. "It's probably buried in one of these boxes. I haven't had a chance to unpack everything—it's been crazy in here!"

She's not kidding. The shelves are practically empty, and there are at least a dozen boxes.

"Maybe it's in this one," she says, tugging open a box flap.

"Mind if we check a few too?" I ask.

"Sure," she replies, heading back to the front. "Excuse me for a minute."

Jordyn and I look at each other. And at the exact same time, we say, "Power time!"

We share a quick thought. Instantly, golden stars shimmer through the room. The boxes practically open themselves, and one by one, perfectly folded tee shirts float into place.

I find the tee shirt we need, the shelves look amazing, and all the boxes are stacked neatly in the corner.

We head to the register, pay for everything, and grab our bag.

Just as we're about to leave, the salesgirl, now helping another customer, calls out, "Did you find another medium?"

"Yeah. Thanks!" I reply, knowing she's going to be shocked when she sees the back room.

She smiles and waves goodbye.

"We totally made her day," Jordyn says, grinning as we step outside.

"Definitely!" I nod. The sun hits our bag just right, and it sort of glows. But as we walk down the sidewalk, my smile fades just a little.

I just wish we could make Dad's day by finally catching Billy and getting him in trouble already.

Jordyn

Blair yells over the noise of kids splashing in the pool, "Jordyn, your art is blowing up on my app! So many people are asking for your advice."

"No way!" I grin, rubbing sunscreen on my legs. "That's so cool—I gotta check it out."

Alix, sitting between us, turns to me. "Congrats!"

"That's lit," Jackson adds just as my cousins show up.

"Pull up some more chairs," Alix says, scooting over.

They grab two chairs and drag them next to us.

"I think it's the hottest day of the week!" Joy sighs, sticking her toe into the water. "Anyone want to go swimming?"

"Yeah," Jackson says. "C'mon, Jordyn!"

"Not yet," I say, still scrolling through all the comments on Blair's app. I'll reply later, but wow—people are actually asking for my advice. Love that for me. Yay!

Splash! Jackson dives right in.

"Hey, does anyone want to see our new dance?" Vicki asks.

"We could use the practice," Kathy chimes in. "An influencer wants to post it soon."

We all sit up. "Absolutely!" I say. Jackson and Joy swim to the poolside.

Kathy hits play on a song from her playlist. The music starts booming, and our cousins start dancing. Everyone gathers around to watch, even the noisy kids.

As the song ends, everyone's cheering and clapping. Someone yells, "Encore!"

Our cousins start dancing again, and everyone's having a blast. Even the fancy lady is doing her ballet moves.

When they finish, everyone goes back to their seats, and some jump in the pool. The fancy lady waves over a cabana boy and asks for an umbrella. Then Billy strolls in, wearing his backpack and carrying a tray of food.

I send a quick thought to Alix: *The crook just showed up!*

She sends her thought back instantly: *I'm not taking my eyes off him.*

The cabana boy tugs at the umbrella, trying to open it. POP! The tip jabs Billy's backpack, and—Oh. My. God—it rips wide open. A diamond ring. Cash. Everywhere. Billy loses his balance, and the tray of food goes flying.

The fancy lady gasps. "My diamond!" She clutches the ring and hurriedly slides it back onto her finger.

Alix and I lock eyes. *Woo-hoo!*, I send to her.

"Billy's a thief!" Blair shouts loud enough for everyone to hear.

His face goes pale, and his lip starts to tremble. I fire off a quick text to Dad while Alix scoops up the money. The entire pool deck goes totally silent—everyone's just staring.

A minute later, Dad rushes in with two policemen.

Billy lets out this defeated sigh, drops his head, and doesn't even fight it as the cops snap the handcuffs on him. Alix hands the cash to Dad, and the crowd starts to break up.

Alix and I look at each other, and she flashes me a thumbs-up. I grin and send one right back. Finally—it's over.

****

Alix

Jordyn and I are hanging in our suite, scrolling on our phones, when Dad walks in.

"It turns out Billy saw the code when his Uncle Axel took money out of the safe one day," Dad says, rubbing his face. He looks exhausted, but there's relief in his voice now that the investigation is over. "After that, he started sneaking money whenever he got the chance."

"Billy getting caught is the best news!" I say.

"Definitely!" Jordyn chimes in.

Dad nods. "I think he'll be in big trouble for a long time. Axel was shocked that it was his nephew."

"I bet!" Jordyn says.

"But you know what? You two really stepped up, and helped catch Billy," Dad says.

"We're always on our toes!" Jordyn says, striking a goofy spy pose.

I laugh.

Dad chuckles. "I'm proud of you both. But I've got to lock up the kitchen, and you two need to get some sleep." He gives us one last smile before gently closing the door behind him.

Jordyn flops on to her bed with a grin. "Maybe now we can come back next year."

"That would be cool!" I say, just as my cell dings. I look down and my heart skips a beat.

"What's up?" Jordyn asks, tilting her head.

"Hold up!" I text Blair, my hands all sweaty.

"You okay, Alix?"

I swallow hard. "Blair's family had to cut their vacation short. She's getting on a plane right now." I pause. "Something about her dad's company being investigated. I don't completely understand, but it sounds serious. Really serious."

Jordyn's eyes widen. "Wait—so no lunch tomorrow?"

I shake my head. "We were supposed to hang out one last time before she left. Now I won't even get to say goodbye."

"You can FaceTime her if you want," Jordyn says softly.

"It's not the same!"

I know Blair's dealing with a lot—her parents, the whole company thing, and who knows what else. It just makes me feel really sad. I wanted to see her one more time.

DAY ELEVEN
AFTERNOON
Jordyn

Alix and I are hanging at the beach while our cousins splash around in the ocean. I'm texting Jackson, who's waiting at the airport.

"Jackson made the spring team!" I tell Alix, bouncing with excitement.

"The last time I was here, I was with Blair," Alix says, looking all mopey.

"Hello? Jackson made the spring team!" I repeat.

Alix sighs, gazing at the ocean. "I finally found my kindred spirit—and now she's gone."

"Seriously? Do you have to be so dramatic?" I roll my eyes. "It's our last day here. We leave tomorrow. Blair doesn't live on the moon. You'll see her again."

"Who knows?" Alix mutters. "We're both busy with school and everything."

I scoop up a handful of sand and let it fall through my fingers. "I bet Mom and Dad will let you visit her. It's not that far."

"Yeah, right," Alix grumbles, kicking at the sand.

I know she's bummed, but she'll have plenty of time to sulk back in freezing Connecticut. "C'mon, let's go for a swim," I say, brushing sand off my legs.

Right as we stand up, I notice a bunch of tiny crabs crawling near my towel. "Ewww!" I scream, jumping back.

Alix looks down and shrieks, "Gross!"

"I don't want them near us!" I shout.

"Me neither," Alix says, her eyes lighting up. "Power time!"

We exchange a quick thought and get ready to use our powers. But suddenly, I hear a voice in my head: *Move them into the ocean.*

"What's happening?" I ask, staring at Alix.

"You heard it too?" she says, eyebrows raised. "Doesn't it sound like—Vicki?"

I whip around—and sure enough, our cousins are standing right behind us. Vicki's casually playing with her crystal necklace.

"WHAAT?!" My brain is spinning. "You guys have the powers too?"

Vicki grins. "Yep! We found our crystals in Silvia's closet. And then she confronted us. She warned us to be careful with our powers."

"Unbelievable!" Alix's eyes go wide. "We found ours in our grandma's attic, and she confronted us too."

"We keep it a secret," Kathy says. "It's our thing."

"We can't tell anyone either!" Alix adds. "We left our crystal necklaces at home."

We all look at each other —and then just crack up.

I have a million questions buzzing in my head, but before I can ask, Vicki's phone rings. "Oh shoot, we gotta go!" she says. "An interviewer from TikTok is waiting for us. We can't be late."

Vicki gives us a quick hug. "Twin powers rule!"

"Life's way better with these magical powers!" Kathy yells as they take off running.

"Wait! Don't go!" I call after them, but they're already gone.

Alix glances down. "The crabs are gone!"

I look too. "Yep, I guess so," I say, smiling.

Alix

Jordyn and I are packing up when Grandma and Mom FaceTimes us.

"Hi!" we both say.

"Don't forget to pack everything," Mom reminds us. "Check all the drawers."

"Got it!" Jordyn says.

"Have a safe trip. I can't wait to see you," Mom says excitedly. "I have to get back to Ace." She gives a quick wave goodbye.

Grandma comes on and says, "I have a feeling something interesting happened."

"Uh, maybe," Jordyn says, trying not to giggle.

Grandma leans in and her face fills the screen. "We'll talk when you get home." She winks and clicks off.

Jordyn and I burst into laughter.

"I had such a fun time," I say with a sigh. "I'm really going to miss Blair, though."

"This trip was the best," Jordyn says, shoving the diary into her bag.

"We've learned a lot," I add. "Going through tough stuff actually makes you stronger."

"That's true!" Jordyn nods. "Remember my whole orange phase? Total disaster. But honestly, it helped. I realized it doesn't matter what anyone else thinks. I just have to be okay with me. I think I'm officially wiser now."

"Absolutely." I smile.

Jordyn grins. "Whatever comes our way—we've got this!"

"We're the fearless Twintastic Twins!" I shout.

"Unstoppable!" Jordyn agrees just as Dad walks in—looking sharp and freshly shaven.

"Hi Dad! You look great!" we say in perfect twin sync.

He chuckles. "Good evening girls. I have some news."

"What's up?" Jordyn asks.

"Looks like we won't get to see your cousins before we leave," Dad says. "They've got TikTok interviews in Boca Raton. But Silvia promised they'll visit soon."

"Bummer!" Jordyn says.

"But—I've got some great news," Dad says with a big smile. "The D Hotel has locations all over the world."

"Wait—like a chain?" Jordyn asks.

"That's right. And even though Axel and I don't always see eye to eye, he gave me credit for my cooking and for helping catch Billy," Dad says.

We lean in, waiting for more.

"He invited me to be a guest chef during spring break and told me to definitely bring my daughters along."

"Cool!" I say. "Where?"

"New York City!" Dad announces.

"No way!" Jordyn and I scream together, throwing our arms around him.

"We're talking museums, Central Park, and the Yankees—the works!" Dad says, pulling out a stack of food containers.

"I can't wait!" I say, feeling excited. "And I'll get to see Blair soon enough!"

"It's going to be terrific," Dad says. "But for now, I have to get going and tie up some loose ends in the kitchen. I'll be back later." He heads out, humming I love New York.

Just as Jordyn and I sit down to eat, another surprise pops up.

"Check this out!" Jordyn shoves her phone in my face. "It's a DM from our cousins."

I look at the screen, and then— "What?!!" I scream.

"They have the *Magical Powers for Twins, Volume TWO!*" Jordyn shouts.

"More powers! More adventures! This is huge!" I yell.

"We have to get the book," I say, grinning.

"Like, ASAP—ASAP!" Jordyn says.

Who could've imagined a Volume Two? Things are about to get even more *Twintastically* epic!